Earthquake Surprise

A Bailey Fish Adventure

Linda Salisbury

Drawings by Carol Tornatore

Tabby House

Cover design and illustrations: Carol Tornatore
Second printing 2013

ISBN-13: 978-1-881539-65-0
ISBN-10: 1-881539-65-2
ISBN-E: 1-881539-66-7

Library of Congress Control Number: 2012934935

Illustration of the representation of the box from Henry
Box Brown's narrative reproduced on p. 185 with permission, from Documenting the American South, the Univer-
sity of North Carolina Chapel Hill Libraries.

Manufactured within CPSIA guidelines.
Printed by Victor Graphics, Baltimore, Maryland
Batch #1

baileyfish@gmail.com
www.BaileyFishAdventures.com
Facebook: AuthorLindaSalisbury

Classroom quantities and
Teacher's Guides available.

Tabby House
P.O. Box 544, Mineral, VA 23117
(540) 895-9093

Contents

1

August 23, 2011

It was the longest bus ride home. Ever!

Even though the afternoon sun was hot, Bailey shivered as she slid into her seat. It felt strange not to have her heavy book bag filling her lap. Her books and homework were still at school. There had been no time to get them, or her art project, when the brick middle school was evacuated.

First the loud, scary noise. Then the desks shook violently in her lower-level classroom, then the walls. Books, a TV, and a gray filing cabinet fell. Bailey clung to her desk and stared at her substitute teacher, who looked puzzled, then fearful. Mrs. Welton steadied herself as the floor felt like a wave passed under it. The students were too surprised to scream. Then they heard the fire alarm, the signal to get outside.

Seconds after the thundering rumble rocked the building, Mrs. Welton lined up her class against the interior wall. "Everyone be quiet and follow me," she said. "Stay calm. We'll be okay." She was acting calm, but her face was tight with concern.

Just a minute earlier Mrs. Welton had been smiling and explaining the math homework. Bailey had glanced at the digital wall clock, which read 1:50 PM.

What had happened? Had a train gone off its tracks across the highway? Was there a plane crash at the nearby airport?

"Stay in a line next to the wall," said Mrs. Welton. "Move quickly, but no shoving." The class followed her. The hall was crowded as sixth-graders looked for their friends and some pushed to get through the doors that led outside toward the parking lots and football field. Kids cried and hugged each other.

What was going on?

"Earthquake," Justin Rudd muttered as his class filed past Bailey's.

"Aliens," said the boy behind him. He had a bounce in his step as though he thought the earthquake was something exciting.

"It's not funny, Rocco," said Bailey's friend, Emily. She had moved up the line to be near Bailey and clutched her arm.

Earthquake? Earthquake? In Virginia?

Bailey tried to focus on that crazy possibility. Earthquakes happened in California, Japan, Haiti, New Zealand, Chile, and in Costa Rica where her mother was living. But in the middle of Virginia in the middle of the day? In the middle of math?

"I'm scared," whimpered Emily. "What if the building falls into a big crack?"

"Shhh," said Bailey. She was afraid, too, but she didn't want to talk to anyone until they were safely outside.

Mrs. Welton marched them into the parking lot away from the building. Bailey blinked in the hot sunlight. It looked like a normal day, but nothing was normal. She watched the high school students streaming out of their building across the field and parking lots.

"Be calm, people," said Mrs. Welton, again. "Please stay with me."

The students were told to sit on the pavement while the teachers took roll. Bailey listened nervously, hoping all the kids she knew were accounted for.

"Hey, my stupid cell phone isn't working," grumbled Shawn. "My dad's going to be worried. I'm supposed to text him if there's ever a problem." Shawn shook his cell phone, then banged it on his knee.

"What if our houses fell down? What if someone's hurt?" Emily grabbed Bailey and choked back tears. "I want to go home."

Home. A ball of panic hit Bailey in the stomach. *Sugar. Oh, my gosh! I wonder if Sugar, and Goldie and the cats are okay. And the Keswicks.* She pushed her light brown hair behind her ears and looked around.

The pavement was so hot that the students were moved to the grass near the football field. Bailey wondered if Sugar would come to get her or if she would have to take the bus home.

A few parents who lived near the schools had already driven into the parking lot and were shouting for their kids. *I wish someone would come for me*, thought Bailey. She recrossed her legs and leaned back on her hands. Even the grassy ground felt hot.

"Look at that," said Justin, pointing at the jet airplane contrails crossing above them in clear blue sky. "It's a big X. Weird. I guess X marks the spot. Mineral."

"Aliens," said Rocco under his breath. He grinned.

2

Damage at home

Fred and Noah Keswick were standing at the end of Sugar's driveway. Bailey gave Emily a quick hug, bolted down the bus steps, and ran to where the boys were waiting for her.

"Where are Sugar and Goldie? Is everyone okay?" yelled Bailey.

"Sugar's at the Book Barn. She wants you to meet her there. Don't go in your house just yet," said Fred.

"Why? What happened?" Bailey searched their faces for answers. The adopted brothers looked excited but worried.

"Lots of things fell down at your house, including part of the chimney, so it's a big mess," said Noah.

"It's worse at our house," said Fred. "Mom was canning tomatoes and the pot lifted off the stove during the earthquake and red sauce went everywhere and burned her hand. I think we'll have the sauce that didn't spill for the next few days." He forced a laugh.

"Where's Goldie? What about the animals?" Bailey's voice quavered. Her hazel eyes burned with salty tears that threatened to fall.

"C'mon," said Fred. "You'll see. Your cats are hiding somewhere. Mom's checking on the horses, but we think they're all okay. You should have seen them run during the quake."

"Traveller was prancing and jumping around a few minutes before the quake happened. Maybe he felt it coming," added Noah.

"What about Goldie?" Bailey looked around, wishing her gentle hound had followed the boys to the bus stop to greet her.

"She'll be glad to see you," said Fred, not really answering Bailey's question. Bailey was going to ask again, but the boys turned and walked quickly up the driveway to Sugar's house, where Bailey had lived since winter.

At first glance, the house looked the same as it had when Bailey had left for school that very ordinary morning. Bailey had stuffed her lunch in her knapsack while her grandmother had reminded her that they would help Miss Bekka with the canning after school. Then later they were invited for dinner at Keswick Inn to celebrate Mr. Will's birthday.

"And it's such a lovely day," Sugar had said. "Perfect for walking through the woods to the Book Barn, right, Goldie?" Bailey's dog had thumped her tail. "I have several boxes of books to unpack."

Bailey had given Sugar a hug before dashing out the front door. She had turned and seen Sugar waving from the porch. Everything was so normal. So ordinary, just like any other school day.

Now Bailey noticed bricks scattered on the ground from the toppled chimney and a large crack in the foundation. The flowerpots that had been on the porch railing had fallen. The porch swing was caught in Sugar's rocker.

"C'mon, Bailey," called Noah.

Instead of following the boys through the backyard to the path between their houses, Bailey ran up the back porch steps.

"Hey, you're not supposed to go inside," called Noah. "It might be dangerous."

"I just want to look," said Bailey. She peered through the glass in the kitchen door. All the cupboards were open and glasses, dishes, cans, and spices had fallen out. She looked through the dining room window. The pictures were crooked and Sugar's hutch, with all her fragile antiques dishes, had fallen over and crashed into the dining room table. Pieces of glass and pottery covered the table and floor. *This is terrible. Sugar will be so sad to see that her grandmother's teacups are smashed,* thought Bailey.

"Let's go," called Fred. "Sugar'll be worried if we don't show up soon."

Bailey's heart was pounding. She wondered if Sallie and Shadow were hiding in the house or under the porch. She called, "Kitty, kitty." If they were outside, they were too afraid to come out. She called again, but there was no sign of the young cats.

She froze when another rumble shook the ground, then ran after her friends who were almost to the woods.

"Hey, did you feel that aftershock?" asked Fred, looking at his watch. "It's the second one since the earthquake. Dad says we could get them for months." He pushed his glasses higher on his nose.

"Really?" Bailey trembled.

"But they probably won't be as strong as the earthquake," said Noah. He broke into a jog.

"Is everyone okay at your house?" asked Bailey, hurrying to catch up.

"Mom's hand was scalded when hot tomato sauce spilled, but nobody else was hurt. Our house is a mess though," said Noah, "and Sparrow is so scared that she stopped talking again."

"Why?" asked Bailey, still having trouble imagining what had happened in her neighborhood just a few hours earlier.

"We were taking a break from homeschool homework, and Sparrow went to her room. Mom went to the kitchen to stir her sauce. Then we heard the most incredible noise," said Noah.

"Dad was afraid the nuclear power plant had blown up. Everything was falling and the walls seemed to bend and sway," said Fred, slightly out of breath.

"We heard Mom calling us and shouting for Sparrow, but Sparrow didn't answer," said Noah, slowing down.

"What happened to her?" asked Bailey.

"Sparrow slid out of her wheelchair and was trying to hide in her closet, but everything had fallen on top of her—all her shoes and toys," said Fred.

"Oh no!" said Bailey, worried about their seven-year-old foster sister.

"She was all right, but she closed her eyes and won't say anything, just like she acted when she first came here," said Noah.

Poor little Sparrow. I don't blame her for being so afraid, thought Bailey.

The closer they got to Keswick Inn, the more Bailey's worries grew. *Why haven't they answered my questions about Goldie?*

3

Where's Goldie?

When they reached the orchard behind Keswick Inn, Bailey stopped for a moment to try to figure out what was going on.

The boys' mother, Miss Bekka, was in the pasture with the skittish horses, calling their names and offering pieces of apple. Mr. Will was checking for cracks in the foundation of the inn. Bailey couldn't see little Sparrow in her wheelchair, nor did she see her grandmother or Goldie.

Noah and Fred had dashed ahead without her and had climbed over the fence to help their mother calm the rescue horses that were still nervously pacing in the field.

Sugar and Goldie must be in the Book Barn. Bailey ran to the small barn that her grandmother was turning into a used bookstore. She yanked at the door, which seemed jammed. Hot worry tears filled her eyes again.

"Is that you, Bailey? Hold on, I'll help," said her grandmother from inside. "The door's been hard to open since the quake. I think the foundation shifted a little."

Together, they forced the door open and Bailey fell into Sugar's arms. A sob escaped before she could stop it.

"It's okay, dear heart," said Sugar.

"I'm so glad you're all right," said Bailey, "but where's Goldie? Noah and Fred wouldn't tell me anything."

"Goldie's going to be fine. She's quite the brave dog," said Sugar, holding her tightly.

"Going to be fine? Where is she?" Bailey pulled away from her grandmother and ran to Goldie's bed in the store. It was covered with pictures that had fallen, and broken glass that glittered in the afternoon sun.

Bailey grabbed Sugar. "This is terrible. Where's Goldie? What happened?"

"She's fine and it's quite a story. Let's go outside where we can sit and talk about our day," said her grandmother. "We'll finish cleaning up later."

Sugar ushered her to a wooden bench near the store's front door. "Do you want to start? I need to hear about what happened to you at school." Sugar looked as dazed as Bailey felt.

"No," said Bailey. "You talk first." She felt Sugar's arm rest on her shoulders, as if to comfort her, and maybe herself.

"Okay. Goldie and I had a splendid walk through the woods this morning, and I unpacked and shelved the new books. Had my lunch and decided to read one of the history books I recently bought. Goldie was sleeping on her bed, but suddenly she sat up and whined. She came over and nudged me and barked, grabbed my hand and pulled me toward the door. I thought she was just playing and so I didn't move right away." Sugar paused. She ran her hand through her short, dyed-brown hair.

"Then what?" Bailey asked impatiently.

"Goldie was so insistent that I finally got up and went to the doorway. Just then the earthquake happened. I jumped out the door. I thought Goldie was right behind me but she was scared and ran back inside. She cut her paw on broken glass from a picture that fell."

"How bad was it? " Bailey jumped up.

"Goldie's going to be fine. We quickly wrapped her paw and fortunately our good friend Hayseed Muckle was on his way to the vet with his dog, whose paw was also injured. So he took Goldie with him so that all the slivers of glass could be carefully removed. That's why I didn't come to get you at school. Don't look so worried, sweetheart. It's a deep cut, but Goldie will be running around soon."

"Can I see her?"

"Hayseed said he'd call when the vet is done but she may need to spend the night. Now, tell me all about what happened at school. You must have been very frightened."

Bailey nodded.

"I want to hear your story, and then we have lots to do," said Sugar, "and it starts with Sparrow."

4

Sparrow

Bailey wanted to go in the big barn to check on her horse, Polly, but Sugar was adamant that they first spend time with Sparrow. They found the little girl on the back porch where Mr. Will had wheeled her for safety. Sparrow was hunched over with her small hands covering her face.

Sugar pulled a rocking chair next to her and said softly, "I'll bet you were pretty scared. I was, too."

"So was I," said Bailey. "I didn't know what was going on when the rumbling started." She pulled a stool near Sparrow's wheelchair.

"None of us knew," said Sugar, "and then everything started falling. What a mess!"

Sparrow nodded.

"Did you get knocked on your noggin?" asked Sugar. She reached over and parted Sparrow's long, dark-blond hair. "Hmm. It looks like there's a bit of a bump. Well, not everyone has an earthquake bump. All the kids will want to see it. It's special."

Sparrow's hands dropped to her lap and she looked at Sugar. She thought for a minute, then touched the tiny lump.

"Really?" she whispered.

"Really," said Bailey. "I'd like to see it."

Sparrow bent down so that Bailey could have a look. "That's amazing," said Bailey. "I don't know anyone else who has one."

"I'm still afraid," said Sparrow.

"The earthquake was very frightening, but it's over and you're safe," said Sugar. "We're all safe."

"What about Sneakers? Is my pony safe? Did the barn fall down?" Sparrow asked.

"I think we should go see," said Sugar. She turned the little wheelchair so that Sparrow was facing the barns. "See, the barns are just fine. We'll be able to get most everything fixed."

Sparrow pushed her hair back and squeezed Bailey's hand.

"And, Sparrow, I'm going to need help in the Book Barn after we get your room straightened up. Can I count on you?" asked Sugar.

The little girl nodded. Sugar pushed her wheelchair down the ramp and onto the path to the big barn where Noah and Fred were feeding the horses after they had coaxed them in from the pasture.

Sneakers stuck his shaggy white head out of his stall when he heard Sparrow call his name. She rubbed his velvety nose and tried to show him her earthquake bump, but the pony snorted and shook his head.

Bailey slipped into Polly's stall and rubbed the horse that the Keswicks were letting her call her own. "Good girl," said Bailey, relieved that the large animals were unhurt. *They must have been terrified along with everyone else when the earthquake happened.* "I'll be back, Polly," said Bailey. She closed the stall door and turned to walk back outside.

"Oh, there you are," said Miss Bekka, coming out of the tack room where the saddles were stored. Her denim shirt and shorts were splattered with red sauce and her right hand was wrapped in gauze. "I could sure use help cleaning up the kitchen if we're going to have a birthday supper tonight."

"Sure," said Bailey. She followed the boys' mother to the house. She wondered what kind of mess she'd see in there.

"Will says he thinks it's safe for us to be in the house, but we'll have a lot of work to do. I'm glad we aren't expecting any guests for a while," said Miss Bekka.

Even though Bailey had looked through the porch window at the inn, she hadn't realized how bad the mess was inside.

Sugar swept up the broken pieces of canning jars and had filled large pans with soapy water. "You can wipe down the cabinets and countertops, while I work on mopping," she said to Bailey. "Bekka can't get her bandage wet."

"The boys can work on the bedrooms when they come in," said Miss Bekka. "I'll see about what's fallen in the living room and dining room."

After Miss Bekka left the kitchen, Bailey asked Sugar, "What about our house and the Book Barn?"

"I know it's a mess at home, but neighbors first," said Sugar. "I'm sure they'll help us later."

5

Gooey gooey cake

At dinner, Miss Bekka joked about her earthquake spaghetti sauce, and said she hoped she never had to fix another batch like that. She said that the birthday cake that she had baked in the morning for Mr. Will had slipped off the table during the earthquake and was such a crumbled mess mixed with red sauce and broken glass, that she couldn't serve it.

"I'll bake you another," she told him, her eyes twinkling, "but in the meantime, here's a gooey gooey substitute."

His green eyes danced when he saw the candle in the bowl of chocolate fudge frosting that was supposed to have been spread on top of the layer cake.

Sparrow laughed for the first time since the earthquake when Mr. Will blew out his candle and passed the bowl of frosting to everyone at the table.

"I like this cake the best ever. I want one for my birthday," Sparrow said, taking a big spoonful, and then another.

The party was fun, but Bailey wasn't the only one who missed Goldie. The Keswicks' little white dog, Clover, whined and went to the door twice, as if she expected Goldie to show up. Bailey wondered if Goldie thought she was being punished by staying in a cage at the animal hospital. She wished she could be there to comfort her.

She looked where the clock used to be, forgetting that it had fallen and now needed repair. Bailey wasn't sure what time it was, but hoped they wouldn't stay long. There was so much to do at home to straighten up their own house.

She offered to help with the dishes, but Miss Bekka said, "No need for that. I know you want to get going. Will has a work list for tomorrow, and I'm coming up with special projects for homeschool."

"Aww, Mom," said Noah. "Can't we have a few days off, like public school?"

"Not in my school," said Miss Bekka, "but the topic should be of interest. I've decided we'll learn about earthquakes. Perhaps Bailey and Justin and his sisters will join us."

"I'd like that," said Bailey.

"Maybe we ought to study hurricanes and tornadoes, too," said Fred. "I heard a hurricane is headed our way."

"Okay, we'll call it a unit on natural events," said Miss Bekka. "Tomorrow will be a day off, though. Boys, you've got kitchen duty tonight. And be careful. We can't afford to have more dishes break."

Mr. Will stood up and said, "I want you all to know this has been a birthday to remember. I think we should celebrate every year with a bowl of frosting."

"My turn to fix it next year," said Sugar. "I make an awesome buttercream."

6

Lucky

Sugar was surprisingly quiet on the drive home from Keswick Inn. She looked tired and worried even though she had assured everyone that she and Bailey would be fine.

Sugar and Mr. Will had walked through her house before Bailey came home from school. Despite the mess from broken dishes and mirrors, fallen lamps, books, and bricks from the chimney, Mr. Will said Sugar's house was safe to stay in. Miss Bekka tried to talk them into staying at Keswick Inn for the night, but Bailey was glad that Sugar was ready to go home. She wanted to see the damage in their house for herself and to find her cats before dark.

Bailey missed Goldie. She wished her dog was sitting on the floor of Sugar's pickup. She wanted Goldie to spend the night in her room, but Sugar and the veterinarian thought that Goldie should stay over to make sure she didn't chew the bandage off. "Besides, we'll get all the glass cleaned up tomorrow so she won't hurt another paw," said her grandmother.

Bailey knew Sugar was right, but it didn't stop her from worrying about Goldie and missing her.

Sugar parked the pickup under a large oak tree near the back porch. Bailey peered through the twilight and exclaimed, "Look!"

Shadow and Sallie were waiting on the top step. Gray Shadow arched his back in a stretch, then bounded down the steps to greet Bailey. Black and white Sallie waited on the porch.

"Kitties, kitties," said Bailey. "I was so worried. I bet you're hungry." She petted them both, glad to hear their purrs.

Bailey followed Sugar through the kitchen door and Sugar turned on the lights. The kitchen was a mess just as Bailey had seen through the window, but it wasn't as bad as the Keswicks' house had been. She walked through the downstairs with her grandmother.

"It's more amazing to me," said Sugar, "at what didn't fall and break than what did." She pointed at a fragile glass vase on a bookshelf and her tall grandfather clock. "Now why didn't they fall over when the books and lamp next to them did? We're very lucky."

Lucky? Bailey had only been looking at what had been broken or damaged, not all the treasures that had survived. Now she wanted to see her room.

"Wow!" she said. All the pictures of the Wild Women were crooked, as if a giant hand had tipped them. *They could have fallen, but they didn't.* Her desk lamp was on the floor. *It could have broken, but it didn't.* There was a crack in the plaster, but only a small piece of wall had

fallen near her dormer window. *I'm lucky.*

Suddenly there was another loud, thundery rumble, like the one that had shaken the school that afternoon. Bailey ran out of her room.

"Was that another earthquake?" she asked Sugar.

"It was just an aftershock. A big one. I don't think we need to worry, though."

They heard a crash above them. Bailey jumped. "What's that?"

"I don't know. We'll check the attic tomorrow," said Sugar. "But now, I've cleared books off the chairs in the library and I think we need to have popcorn and sweet tea while we return phone calls. We have messages from all over. Everyone wants to know if we're okay. Cleanup can wait until morning."

The aftershock rattled Bailey more than the earthquake. She couldn't figure out why. Maybe it was because she now knew that earthquakes were possible in Central Virginia. Maybe it was because she didn't know what would happen to the house if there was a big aftershock or lots of little ones.

"Do you want to sleep in my room tonight?" her grandmother asked. "It's okay with me if we have a slumber party."

Bailey thought about it for a minute, then decided she'd rather be in her own bed, but she slept fitfully. She missed having Goldie curled up next to her. She missed hearing Sugar's cuckoo clock, which had crashed during the quake. She worried that something might still fall on her. Worry covered her like a heavy blanket. She was glad when she heard her grandmother walking around downstairs. She looked at her alarm clock. It was morning, even though it was still dark.

7

Earthquake surprise

Sugar was sipping her second cup of coffee when Bailey found her in the kitchen reading the morning paper. "The quake was felt in thirteen states," Sugar said. "A lot of damage in Washington, D.C., and all over."

Bailey peered over her shoulder to look at pictures of damage to buildings in the nation's capital and far north. People had felt the earthquake in the Midwest, in the South and as far away as Maine. "You see, it's not just us, even though we were near the epicenter where it began," said Sugar. "Now, as soon as you're ready, we'll check the attic."

Bailey quickly finished a piece of toast and glass of orange juice. If Goldie were home, she would have given her fresh kibble and let her run outside for a few minutes.

"I'm ready for the attic," she said. She followed Sugar upstairs.

Sugar pulled down the folding ladder and climbed to where she could reach the cord for the overhead light. Bailey followed her and gasped when she saw how the attic looked. Boxes had toppled, a bookcase had spilled its contents, Mae, the spy's, red hat box was upside down and a feather from her hat peeked out. The rack of winter coats and sweaters was on its side. Sugar didn't say anything about how bad it looked. Her grandmother pushed her way

through the boxes over to the brick chimney. The earthquake had shaken loose the top, and old bricks had fallen through the roof creating a ragged hole. Part of the attic wall next to the chimney had also been knocked out and a few bricks had tumbled down.

"Oh, my!" said Sugar, peering through the roof where the sky was pale with early morning light. "We knew we had chimney problems, but not about the damage to the roof and this wall." She picked up a brick. "These are wonderful old bricks. Probably made from Virginia clay before the Civil War." She handed it to Bailey.

Bailey felt the rough texture and tried to imagine people making them more than 160 years earlier. She placed it back with the other bricks and looked closely at the jagged hole. She saw that a floorboard had come loose when falling bricks had smacked it. Bailey lifted a corner and saw a thin leather string, no thicker than a shoelace. She gave it a tug, but it only moved a tiny bit. It seemed to be attached to something larger. She pulled on the board and saw that the string was connected to an object that looked like a flat wallet. She pulled again, gently this time. Out came a little book wrapped in soft, reddish-brown leather, the color of an autumn maple leaf. The rest of the string was tied securely around its middle. Bailey cradled the little book in her hands.

"Sugar, look at what I found." She couldn't contain her excitement.

Her grandmother stumbled into a plastic bin stuffed with papers as she hurried over. Bailey carefully handed her the little book. She watched Sugar's face crinkle into a huge smile.

"We never would have found this treasure if it hadn't been for our earthquake," said Sugar.

"Whose is it?" asked Bailey.

"We'll find out when we examine it downstairs in more light," said Sugar. "Did you find anything else in its hiding place?"

Bailey turned quickly and stuck her hand back under the floorboard. She felt the rough wood and a sharp nail. She was about to give up the search when her fingers touched cloth. "I found something else," she said.

"Let me help," said Sugar. "I'll pull up that board." She placed the little book on a nearby carton and with both hands helped Bailey tug at the floorboard until, with a wooden groan, the board let go and popped out.

Bailey's eyes opened wide. She knelt down for a closer look. "What is it, Sugar?"

"Another earthquake surprise," her grandmother said.

8

Hidden treasures

Sallie and Shadow were waiting by the back door when Bailey and her grandmother returned to the kitchen. "I guess it's light enough to let them out," said Sugar. The cats quickly slipped outside into the warm morning air.

Sugar covered the kitchen table with a clean white cloth to protect the fragile attic treasures.

"What shall we look at first?" asked Sugar after heating up her coffee in the microwave.

"The book," said Bailey, "because that's what we found first."

"My choice, too," said Sugar. Her soft, freckled hands worked on the tight knot in the leather strap, while Bailey leaned in for a closer look. The little book reminded her of one she had seen displayed at a museum.

"There," Sugar said. She opened the covers. "It may be a little diary or day book."

"But whose?" Bailey was having trouble reading the tiny words written in faint brown ink.

"Let's see. There's a date and initials. I'll need my magnifying glass."

"I'll get it," said Bailey.

"Later," said Sugar. "I think it's in the library under books that fell yesterday. We'll have to move things to get to it. Let's look at the little box."

The cloth bag was the color of coffee with cream and had a rough texture, like it was intended to protect whatever was carried inside. The little wooden box was about the size of a paperback book and was fastened with a rusty clasp. Sugar carefully opened it and lifted the lid. She pulled out several pieces of folded paper.

"That's all?" Bailey was disappointed.

"Not exactly," said Sugar, reaching deeper inside the box. "Here's something else." She held out a large, well-polished horse chestnut.

"A nut? Why would anyone save a big brown nut?" Bailey asked.

"There's got to be a reason. This one is shiny, like someone carried it in a pocket and rubbed it for luck, or to hide feelings, such as worry," answered Sugar. She handed the chestnut to Bailey.

Bailey turned it over in her palm, wondering about the person who had owned the chestnut and why it had been hidden along with the papers and diary in the attic. What did it mean?

Sugar turned her attention to the papers, yellowish-brown with age. She slowly unfolded one. "Mmm," said Sugar. "It looks like a simple map. I'm not sure of what."

The second paper showed a sketch of a crate. The third was a drawing of starburst with a box in the center.

"I think it is a quilt pattern. I hope the diary gives us clues to the mystery," said Sugar.

9

Unexpected visitors

"We'll need to find a safe place for these treasures," said Sugar. She looked around the kitchen, "but where? I guess we'll leave them on the table until we straighten up the library."

Bailey glanced at the clock. It was almost six. She wondered how soon they could go for Goldie and bring her home.

On a normal Wednesday at this time she'd be washing her breakfast dishes and getting ready to catch the bus. This was not a normal Wednesday. There would be no school today and maybe not tomorrow, either.

Bailey thought about the things she had left behind in her locker and the classroom. There were extra cookies in her lunch bag, plus her books, homework, and a new picture that her mother, Molly, had e-mailed from Costa Rica.

The picture showed her mom holding a hermit crab she found on a Pacific Ocean beach.

Dr. Andrew Snorge-Swinson, the entomologist she was going to marry, took the picture. Bailey was glad Bug Man, as she called him, wasn't in it. She didn't like looking at his face and long ponytail. She didn't like the way her mother looked at him with such dewy eyes, either.

"When can we get Goldie?" Bailey asked her grandmother.

"I'll call at 7:30 when the animal hospital opens," said Sugar. "Now, let's have a real breakfast for energy. We have a busy day ahead."

Before Bailey could say "scrambled eggs" there was a loud knock.

"Awfully early for company," said Sugar, walking to the door.

"Paul!" she said with obvious surprise.

Paul? That was the name of Bailey's father who lived in Guam with his wife, Flora, and their kids.

"And me, too!" That voice was Norma Jean's—Bailey's half sister whom she had met in the spring. Bailey froze.

"My goodness, what are you doing here?" asked Sugar. "Come in. Come in. We were just going to fix breakfast."

Paul Fish and Norma Jean stepped inside the kitchen. Norma Jean ran over to Bailey and gave her a big hug. "Guess what? We moved to the States last week. We were going to surprise you this weekend, but then there was the earthquake. . . ."

Their father continued, "We're staying at a motel near Dahlgren until we figure out where we want to settle when I start my new job at the base. When we heard about the earthquake, we thought we'd better see if there was anything we could do to help here now."

Norma Jean interrupted, "We actually didn't feel the earthquake because we were driving to a shopping center, but everyone was talking about it in the store."

Sugar hesitated, then smiled. "Sure, that would be wonderful. I could use help on repairs. But first, breakfast. Eggs, toast and homemade blackberry jam and juice. Does that sound good, Norma Jean?" she asked.

There was no answer. Norma Jean had already slipped out of the kitchen and was exploring the house. *Nosy Norma Jean hasn't changed at all*, thought Bailey.

Their father, smiling happily, took a step toward her. Bailey backed away and said, "We're going to get my dog in a few minutes." She hoped he'd get the message that he shouldn't stay long.

The smile left his face and Bailey continued, "Goldie's paw was hurt in the earthquake."

"Sorry about that. I'd like to meet her later," said her father. "We won't be here long this morning—just long enough to check your damage and to see what supplies we might need to buy to fix things. Meanwhile, breakfast sounds wonderful." He pulled out a chair and sat down. "Come sit with me. I haven't seen my Bailey girl in quite a while. You look even more grown-up than the first time we met."

Bailey hesitated, then saw Sugar's face. "Okay," said Bailey, and sat sideways in a chair across from the dad she barely knew. "Hi," she said, gazing at his hazel eyes and hair the color of hers.

"Hi back," he said. "Now that we're moving nearby, we'll really get to know each other."

10

Poor paw

"That was a surprise," said Sugar, after their unexpected company left for Keswick Inn to see what they could do to help there, too. "Frankly, I'm really glad to have Paul's help with the chimney and the roof. Will and the boys have their own work at the inn and they've also said they'd help Justin and his mother patch plaster that cracked."

Bailey followed her grandmother to the pickup and climbed in. She didn't respond.

"Norma Jean said she couldn't wait to meet the Keswicks. They hadn't fixed up the inn and moved in when she visited us in early spring," continued Sugar. She adjusted her sunglasses and started the engine.

Bailey looked out the window. The visit from her father and Norma Jean filled her with gloom. She had only seen pictures of her stepmother, Flora, and her little half brothers. And although e-mails from her dad and Norma Jean had said that they eventually would be coming to the United States, she hadn't expected it to be so soon or without any warning. She just wasn't ready for them. Bailey knew that Norma Jean would weasel her way in with Bailey's friends and then what? She knew she was being selfish, but she didn't feel like sharing the Keswicks with Norma Jean.

Miss Nosy had gone through Sugar's entire house and reported on all the damage and messes in each room when she had returned to the kitchen. She seemed much too glad to see Bailey and kept talking about all the things they would do together now that she would be living closer.

Bailey had tried to be polite, but she wasn't in the mood. She might have been glad to see Norma Jean and their father on Monday, August 22, on a normal day before the earthquake, but not now when there was so much to do and talk about with Noah and Fred, and Sugar. The boys were here when it happened, not Norma Jean. She wasn't part of it.

"Your dad certainly is willing and able to help with repairs," Sugar repeated, without a response from Bailey. Bailey knew her grandmother was hoping that she'd say something positive about their visitors but her mind was focused on Goldie. Her gentle hound, abandoned by a hunter, hadn't been away from her all night since Bailey had adopted her. Poor Goldie. She must be wondering if she had been abandoned again.

As they drove along the country roads Bailey saw many people on ladders looking at their damaged chimneys. Some open holes were already being covered with blue plastic tarps. Bailey wanted to see what was going on in the town of Mineral, where there was damage to the post office, town hall, a lot of businesses, and homes. Sugar said they would drive by later, after they had picked up Goldie.

Three people were in the waiting room of the animal hospital. One had a small dog that was trying so hard to get outside that it looked like it was swimming. The other two had carrying cages with cats inside. Bailey peeked in, and saw shiny eyes and fur.

Sugar paid Goldie's bill and a helper in a green uniform said she'd be right back with the dog. Bailey leaned on the counter. She heard barking. It couldn't be Goldie because her hound was usually very quiet. Then she saw the helper's face through the glass and the door swung open. Goldie cried and limped as fast as she could to Bailey's waiting arms. Goldie held up her bandaged front paw as if she wanted Bailey to see it. The hound's tail thumped wildly.

"Good girl. Poor paw," whispered Bailey, stroking her dog's silky ears. "Ready to go home?"

Goldie didn't waste time hobbling to the door. Bailey and Sugar were right behind her.

Sugar gave the dog a boost into the pickup and Goldie settled happily at Bailey's feet, her head in Bailey's lap.

"I'll fix you a special breakfast," said Bailey, "and you can sleep all day on your bed." She stroked the dog's head where there was a spot the color and shape of a goldie shell.

Goldie sighed.

"It'll be hard to keep her quiet for a day or so," said Sugar, "and Doc wants to see her in a week to take out the stitches, but he say's she'll be fine."

"You were so brave," Bailey said, rubbing Goldie's ears. "I have special treats for you."

Bailey glanced at the clock on the dashboard. On a normal day she'd be in social studies, getting ready for a quiz they were supposed to have on Friday.

"When do you think that we can go back to school?" Bailey asked.

"Not for a few weeks," said Sugar. "I heard on the news this morning that the damage was very bad at the high school and also at Thomas Jefferson Elementary. It was lucky that Fern's class was outside on the playground when the quake hit."

"Why? What happened?" Bailey realized she hadn't asked questions about the experiences of other friends and neighbors. All she had been thinking about was Sugar, Goldie, and the Keswicks.

"I haven't talked to her—just heard what Justin said—so you might want to ask when you see her," said Sugar. "Everyone has a special story." She slowed to turn into their driveway.

"We're home, girl," said Bailey.

When they reached the kitchen, Bailey noticed that the light on the answering machine was blinking. She played the message. Miss Bekka said there would be a potluck at the inn that night, and that she had invited the rest of Bailey's family so that everyone could get acquainted.

Sugar seemed thoughtful when she listened to the message a second time. "We'll get my office and the dining room cleaned up today, and I guess I'll make mac and cheese to take."

Bailey didn't answer. She wasn't ready to meet her stepmother and half brothers.

She filled Goldie's bowl with fresh kibble. "I'd rather stay home with just you," she said, rubbing her dog's head.

11

Meeting family

"It was awfully nice of Bekka and Will to invite us all for dinner when they still have so much work to do at their house," said Sugar.

Bailey noticed that her grandmother had dressed in her best checkered blouse and her nicest denim overshirt and jeans. She had smoothed her hair and even washed the smudges off her glasses.

Bailey wasn't sure how to dress to meet her new family. She finally decided not to wear her newest clothes—the green T-shirt that her mother had just sent from Costa Rica. If they didn't like her in her old clothes, then so what! Sugar glanced at Bailey's frayed cutoff jeans and light-blue T-shirt with the peace sign on it, but didn't say anything.

"Ready?" asked Sugar.

Bailey nodded. She didn't feel ready. She wanted dinner to be over so she and Sugar could come home, sit on their porch, look at the stars, and listen to nature's night songs.

Goldie picked up her leash and hopped to the door.

"She wants to come," said Bailey, half expecting her grandmother to say that there would be enough confusion at dinner and that Goldie should stay home. Instead, Sugar surprised her.

"Goldie is part of our side of the family, don't you think?" Sugar asked.

Bailey gave her grandmother a big hug. It would be so much easier to meet the rest of Norma Jean's family if Goldie were standing next to her. It would be so much easier if these people were *just* Norma Jean's relatives, and not hers, too.

The August air was still sticky hot, reminding Bailey of summer in Florida. Instead of walking through the woods, they drove to make the trip easier for Goldie. Bailey saw a black SUV parked in the Keswicks' driveway. That meant that her father and his family were already there. She petted Goldie's head.

"Everything's going to be fine," said Sugar. "I'll be there with you, and don't forget that I have custody of you while your mom travels."

When they reached the porch, Bailey could hear Norma Jean telling the Keswicks about how she and Bailey had been in their house before it was fixed up.

Sugar opened the screen door and Bailey stepped inside. "Sister," yelled Norma Jean and raced over to hug Bailey. "C'mon, I want you to meet Mom and . . ."

Bailey looked around and saw their father down the hall in the kitchen talking with Mr. Will. Behind Norma Jean was a slender woman with creamy tan skin and black silky hair. She looked just like Norma Jean. She had a slight smile on her face, as if she knew she ought to look friendly. She didn't step toward Bailey and Sugar until her grandmother said, "Flora, we've heard so much about you. You have such a lovely daughter."

"Yes, Norma Jean, Paul's *oldest* daughter is charming," said Flora, in a soft voice. "Thank you for letting her visit with you."

Bailey looked at Sugar. *That isn't right. I'm his oldest daughter, not Norma Jean.*

"I'm Bailey," she announced. She felt Norma Jean's arm around her waist. Flora Fish forced a smile and said, "Nice to meet you," but her words sounded like a chilly breeze had caught them.

Norma Jean dropped her arm and said, "Come out, you guys. Bailey won't bite." She pulled her brothers from behind Flora. "You sillies. Meet your sister," she said.

The little boys' shy smiles were friendly as Norma Jean pulled them to Bailey. Paulie had dark hair, like Norma Jean's, and Sam's was lighter, much like their father's.

The brothers were so quiet that Bailey finally said, "This is Goldie. I hear you have a cat and a dog."

"We had to leave Kee and Kimo in Guam," said Paulie sadly.

"Dad says we can get a new dog when we have a house," said Sam. He sat on the floor where he could wrap his arm around Goldie. "I miss Kimo. He used to sleep with me."

"What happened to her paw?" asked Paulie.

"She hurt it in the earthquake," said Norma Jean. "Remember when we had an earthquake in Guam?"

"Yes, I don't like earthquakes," said Sam.

"Me, neither," said Bailey, "but Sugar says we'll be okay now." She realized that nobody had introduced Sugar, but her grandmother didn't seem to mind. She had walked across the room to talk with Flora, who hadn't moved.

12

After dinner

During dinner Norma Jean chattered away, making Noah and Fred laugh at her stories. Even Bailey had to admit that Norma Jean was funny, especially when she talked about the long flight across the Pacific. She told how her little brothers entertained the other passengers by pretending to be flight attendants serving food in the middle of the night.

Paulie and Sam lost their shyness when they saw Miss Bekka's chocolate cake. It was like the one that had been ruined by the earthquake, and was covered with more of Miss Bekka's delicious fudge frosting.

The boys didn't talk much, but they had wide friendly smiles, like Norma Jean's, that showed all their teeth. Paulie and Sam often looked at Bailey, as if they were trying to figure her out. Bailey didn't know what they had been told about her.

"So, tomorrow, we'll begin with Sugar's chimney and the porch roof," Mr. Will said, "and we'll get the tarps on them. Then we'll start to make repairs here at the inn." He passed the platter of cake slices to Sugar. She placed a piece on her plate, then helped Sparrow select one. Sparrow pointed to the one with the most frosting.

"I'll be here early," said Bailey's dad. "We should be able to get a lot done before I have to report to work next week at the base."

Flora threw down her napkin and pushed her plate away. "Have you forgotten, Paul, that we need to find somewhere to live?" she asked. "A motel is not a good place to raise our children. Finding a home should come first." She sounded both worried and angry.

For a second Bailey felt sorry for her. *It must be hard to move to a foreign land and not have a house of your own.*

"I haven't forgotten," Bailey's father said with a smile. "In fact, Will and I've been talking." He stroked his reddish, pointed beard.

Oh, no! thought Bailey. *I hope they aren't going to live at the inn.*

Norma Jean grinned, like she knew about her father's plan. "This is so cool," she whispered to Bailey.

Paul Fish leaned back in his chair. "We're going to rent the place that Will's mother owns down the road. It's plenty big and has lots of furniture we can use."

"Miss Dolly's house," said Norma Jean happily. "Remember when Bailey and I went there to see her?" Norma Jean sounded like she was going to tell about that visit, but her mother, who looked alarmed, interrupted. "Paul, I thought . . ."

"I know we talked about living near the base, but this will be so much better for all of us to get to know each other, and I don't mind the drive." He smiled at Bailey. "I want my kids to be close."

Flora's lips pushed together as if to keep words she wanted to say from spilling out.

Miss Bekka seemed to sense that something was wrong. She walked over to Bailey's stepmother and placed a hand on her shoulder. "Flora," Miss Bekka said, "I understand you are very artistic. I'm looking for someone to design a special tablecloth for the inn. Perhaps you can help once you get settled. It will be lovely having you as a neighbor. Sparrow will like having your boys to play with."

Flora's face softened for a second when she looked at Miss Bekka. "Thank you, Bekka," she said, but then her expression hardened again. "Paul, we must be going," she said. She stood up so quickly that she knocked over her half-empty glass of sweet tea. "Let's go, children. Hurry. *Bilis*."

"Sure, dear. You must be tired," said Bailey's dad. "We'll be back tomorrow." He blew a kiss to Bailey and thanked the Keswicks and Sugar.

"What's with your stepmother?" Noah asked Bailey after their guests had left. He carried dirty dessert plates to the sink. "She was in a rush to get away from here. 'Hurry. *Bilis*.' I guess that means get-out-of-here-fast in some language. We'll have to ask Norma Jean."

"I don't think Miss Flora likes it here," said Fred.

I don't think she likes me, thought Bailey.

13

Unusual book

Bailey reached over to touch Goldie, but her dog wasn't next to her in the bed. Bailey quickly dressed and hurried downstairs. It was still dark outside. Goldie was sitting in the kitchen waiting for breakfast.

"What are you doing up so early, Sugar?" Bailey asked, rubbing the sleep from her eyes.

"I couldn't sleep. Thought I'd get started straightening up the library before we get busy with other things," said her grandmother.

"I'll help," said Bailey. She poured kibble in Goldie's bowl and grabbed a banana for herself. When she was done eating, Goldie limped after them to the library and flopped on the floor in the doorway.

Sugar said, "I'll start in this corner and you begin over there. We'll get things back on the shelves, and organize them later. It will help me if you dust them as you go, though."

Bailey picked up paperback books that were scattered everywhere, then the hardbacks. Under them were several leatherbound books of different sizes. She selected a small one. "Sugar, look at this! It's really old, like the one we found in the attic."

Sugar gently rubbed the leather cover of the little book. "There were several books on the shelf when I moved here years ago and I was so busy unpacking the rest of my books, I didn't look carefully at them."

"Here's another old one," said Bailey. "The author has a funny middle name. 'Box.'" She opened it and read the title: *Narrative of the Life of Henry Box Brown written by himself.* She turned another page and another. It was an old copy of a book printed in 1851 and there was a short poem that began "Forget not the unhappy / Though sorrow may annoy / There's something then for memory / *Hereafter* to enjoy." *I wonder what that means,* thought Bailey.

"We'll look at that one later, too," said Sugar. She quickly sorted books into several piles.

Bailey placed the book on a low shelf where she could find it again. "How old is your house, Sugar?" asked Bailey. She wrinkled her nose from the dust she brushed off books before standing them again on the shelves.

"According to records, it and the Keswicks' place, were built before the Civil War. Maybe in the 1840s. Maybe earlier. My ancestors—the people who built the house—were farmers. I don't know much more about them."

"Would they be my relatives, too?" Bailey asked.

"Why, yes. My ancestors are your ancestors. That's why it is fun finding out about the past. You never know what you'll learn," said Sugar. "I'll show you the family tree when we find it in all this mess. Your name is on it."

"Sweet," said Bailey. "Do you know about the Keswicks' house?"

"Not much, other than Mr. Will's family—way back—lived there. Their name was Emmett. Mr. Will's grandmother, Miss Dolly, was one of the Emmetts. Her house was built about the same time."

Bailey remembered when she and Norma Jean had had a scary experience in the woods with Miss Dolly, but later they discovered how sweet and nice she could be, and how talented she was. After Miss Dolly died, Bailey was given her old piano so she and Sugar could take lessons. Now Norma Jean and her family would be moving into Miss Dolly's house down the road. Bailey sighed.

"What's the matter, sweetheart?" Sugar asked. "Need a break?"

"No, it's just that . . ." Before she could finish, Sugar's cell phone rang in the kitchen.

"Who could be calling at this early hour? I hope it's not an emergency. I'll be back in a minute," her grandmother said.

14

Too early

Bailey decided to have another look at the old books that were still on the floor. She found a McGuffey's *Eclectic Spelling Book* in which someone named Louise had written "Jan. 17, 1884." There were several alphabets in the book, including fancy script, and one with pictures of animals, such as a quail for Q.

Another tattered book with a green cover was titled *The Young and Field Literary Readers, Book Four* from 1914. Someone named Daniel had signed his name in this one, which was filled with stories. Bailey thumbed through the pages. She found a story by Thomas Nelson Page about "Kittykin and the Part She Played in the War." *Wow!* thought Bailey when she read that the author lived in nearby Hanover County. It was a Civil War story about a kitten that stopped the fighting between Confederates and the Union forces on a little farm near Richmond.

It looked like a good story. Bailey placed the book near the one by Henry Box Brown and the little diary.

"Find something else?" asked Sugar. She returned with her phone and another cup of coffee.

"Yes," said Bailey. "I want to read them later. Who called?"

"Norma Jean," said Sugar, with what sounded like a sigh. "I reminded her that it was very very early to call to chat and that we'd see them later."

"They're *both* coming back today?" Bailey knew she should say "Dad and Norma Jean," but she was still having trouble calling Paul Fish "Dad."

Sugar didn't seem to hear her. Bailey went back to work, carefully dusting, then shelving books. Soon she had uncovered Goldie's puffy fleece pillow between the recliners. "Here's your library bed," she said. Goldie quickly sat up and hobbled to the cushion, her tail wagging. She flopped down happily. "There. We're getting back to normal," said Bailey.

"About another hour and we'll have this room in good shape for now," said Sugar. "Then, we'll go over to the inn and see what we can do there."

15

Earthquake School

"Who's coming to Earthquake School?" Sparrow asked. "Miss Bekka said we need to set up lots of chairs and tables in the living room and I have to count out paper and pencils."

Bailey answered, "You and me, Fred and Noah, Justin, Fern, Daisy, and Martha."

"Daisy and Martha are pretty little," said Sparrow. "What about Norma Jean and your brothers?"

Bailey started to say that they wouldn't be at the school, but then she realized that she really didn't know if that were true. Anything could happen with Norma Jean!

"I'll count stuff for them just in case," said Sparrow.

Bailey wasn't sure how the Earthquake School, as Sparrow named it, was going to work out. Noah, Fred, and Sparrow were accustomed to having school at home with Miss

Bekka. Everybody else rode the bus to public school, but the public schools were closed, at least for a couple of weeks. Sugar had heard that when school started again, the high school and middle school students might share the middle school building and have classes every other day.

Bailey heard clattering and banging down the hall. Fred and Noah appeared with two large folding tables. "Next we get the chairs," said Fred. "Mom said to set up eleven."

Bailey thought, *Oh, no. That means they think that Norma Jean, Paulie, and Sam might be coming, too.*

Miss Bekka bustled into the room carrying an armful of pillows. "These are for the little kids," she said, with a smile. "Did you feel the aftershock this morning, Bailey?"

"I slept through it, but Sugar felt it," she answered.

"I hear voices on the porch," said Miss Bekka. "Would you show everyone where we've set up the school?"

"Sure," said Bailey, happy to be asked to help.

Standing on the porch were Justin, his little sisters, and their mother, Mrs. Rudd. "Are you positive that Miss Bekka wants everyone here today?" Mrs. Rudd asked. She was wearing her Dottie-Anna Restaurant uniform.

"Oh, yes," said Bailey. "Miss Bekka's getting the room ready for school."

"Be good, then," Mrs. Rudd said, kissing the little blond girls. "And you, too, Justin."

Justin shifted on his feet. Bailey wasn't sure he liked the idea of having school at the Keswicks'. She knew he was smarter than he acted. Norma Jean had figured that out when she had visited. She said Justin was really good at making things. She liked him a lot, even when Bailey hadn't.

Bailey looked at her wristwatch. School would start in five minutes and so far no Norma Jean. That was good. Maybe they were moving into their new house today, or shopping. She closed the screen door and pointed toward the living room. The little Rudd girls ran ahead and called for Sparrow.

"Sit with me," said Sparrow. Her wheelchair was parked between two chairs with pillows at a table in the front. Daisy and Martha quickly took seats on either side of her.

Fern found Bailey and asked if she could sit next to her. "Sure. Hey, tell me what happened at Thomas Jefferson Elementary during the earthquake. Sugar said it was scary."

Fern nodded. "Well, we were at recess and I was swinging on the monkey bars, and Lilly and Terry were kicking the soccer ball, and we heard a big noise and everything shook, and the ball rolled away by itself. I fell off the monkey bars and then, when I tried to run, I fell down. The ground was bumping around and the trees were bending. "

"Wow!" said Bailey. "Did you get hurt?"

"Just a little cut on my knee. It didn't hurt though. I was too scared," said Fern. "I don't want to go on the monkey bars ever again."

Bailey hugged her. "It was scary for everybody."

Fern said, "And you know what? After the shaking stopped it got really really quiet. I was afraid something else was coming."

"Tell her about Addie!" said Martha.

"What about Addie?" Bailey had met her friend once at the Rudds' house.

"Oh, she was upstairs in her classroom and the floor started to slant toward the windows and everything was sliding and falling. She got under her desk, but boys pulled her out. Then, she got hit on the head with a piece of the ceiling. She wasn't really hurt, though. She slid along the wall and ran out," said Fern.

"That was real scary," said Martha.

Miss Bekka came back into the room and showed Fred and Noah where to set up the large white board. "There," she said. "I think we're ready to begin. Everyone have a seat."

Bailey was relieved that three chairs in the back were still empty.

16

Class begins

Miss Bekka leaned against the table and welcomed everyone. "Who has seen the little Trevilians school building in Mineral?" A few hands raised. "A hundred years ago there were little schools like that all over the country for grades up to six or seven. Children of all ages went to school together. That's sort of what we have here. I think Daisy is in kindergarten, and Bailey and Justin are in sixth. Fred and Noah are in seventh, so we are the same sort of one-room school."

"Earthquake School," said Sparrow.

"Exactly," said Miss Bekka, with a smile. "We really don't know when some of you'll be going back to public school full time, so let's try to stay busy, and we'll do some fun things together."

Justin groaned, then deliberately squeaked his chair. Bailey jerked around to look at him.

She hoped he wouldn't cause problems just because his mother wanted him to attend with his sisters. Everyone had been getting along pretty well lately but she knew Justin tried to be funny sometimes when a teacher's back was turned.

"I think everyone's interested in learning more about earthquakes. Am I right?" Miss Bekka continued, "How many of you think that this earthquake was the first one ever to happen in this area?" Justin's sisters and Sparrow raised their hands.

"I've been doing a little research and I think we might find surprises. Now, my thought is that we start with a unit on earthquakes. What should we try to discover?"

Soon the whiteboard was filled with a list of ideas—from learning about why there could be an earthquake in Virginia to telling stories about what happened to everybody during the quake. Fred suggested that they each write a story or draw pictures and maybe they could put together a book.

"Excellent idea," said Miss Bekka. "We can start on that today." She suggested that for the first few days they would divide into two groups—older and younger—to work on specific projects.

Fred and Noah said they'd like to research why earthquakes happen, and especially in Virginia. When Miss Bekka asked Justin to get specific information on the August 23 quake and to keep track of the locations of the aftershocks, he shrugged his shoulders and looked out the window.

Bailey agreed to find out about the history of earthquakes in the area.

Sparrow fidgeted and raised her hand. "Miss Bekka, what about earthquake surprises?"

"Great idea," said Miss Bekka. "I wonder what they might be. I think that will be a good topic."

Bailey thought of what she and Sugar had found so far because of the earthquake. When she knew more, it would be fun to share the information with the rest of Earthquake School.

17

Special lunch

During a break for lunch, Bailey dashed over to the Book Barn to see if Sugar needed help.

She was surprised that the little bookstore looked so neat. Books were back on the shelves and the carpet and floors were vacuumed. When she saw Bailey, Goldie whined and wagged her tail, but stayed on her big pillow. Bailey knelt down and rubbed her ears. Goldie lapped her face.

"Looks good, doesn't it?" said her grandmother. "Didn't take as long as I expected, but I had good help from Mr. Will." Sugar plopped down in her recliner. She opened a cooler. "I brought lunch. Tell me about school."

Bailey pulled up a chair next to Sugar's desk and peeked in the cooler. "Yum," she said, taking out a peanut butter and jelly sandwich. "Everybody's writing stories or drawing pictures today, and we have assignments. I have to learn about other earthquakes that may have happened in this area. I don't know how to find out, though," said Bailey.

"I'll be glad to help, if that's okay with Bekka," said Sugar.

"She said it would be all right for everyone to ask grown-ups for help, as long as we wrote our own reports. Just like regular school," said Bailey, taking another big bite.

"Now, if we were going to learn about historic earthquakes, where do you think we should begin?" asked Sugar.

Bailey swallowed and sipped from a water bottle. "Books?"

"Yes, and where else?"

"The Internet?" said Bailey.

"And?"

"The historical society," suggested Bailey.

"All will have answers, some more reliable than others," said her grandmother. "If you have time, check out my Virginia history shelf. Let the investigation begin!"

"First the cookies," said Bailey. "Mine from Tuesday are still in my book bag in my locker. I should have eaten them, but I was in a hurry."

When she was finished, Sugar showed her where the books about Virginia were located. Several were guidebooks to cities or places to visit, but many were old, like the ones Bailey had discovered in Sugar's library. They were hardback and the covers weren't very colorful. Sugar reached for a history of Virginia written long ago. Its pages were yellow and instead of pictures, there were drawings. Sugar handed it to Bailey. "See if it mentions Louisa County."

"No, not really," said Bailey after a few minutes. She looked through several others. "Nothing here either."

"I have a rare one at home that we need to check out tonight," said Sugar. "It was written by a geologist, who traveled through the South before the Civil War and wrote a book about what he learned. I believe he came through this area."

Bailey nodded, but she was only half listening. Another old book had caught her attention. "But wait," she said, "here's one about Richmond that mentions Henry Box Brown. May I borrow it for now?"

"Of course," said Sugar. "That's our other project—to learn about Mr. Box Brown."

"Oh, there's the bell," said Bailey. "Miss Bekka said she'd ring their big old dinner bell to let us know when the afternoon session was starting."

18

More students arrive

Goldie followed Bailey the next morning through the woods to Keswick Inn. The hound still limped but she was putting more weight on her foot. Miss Bekka had said that dogs could come to school as long as they were well-behaved. Bailey knew that Goldie would sleep quietly in a corner or on the porch.

Bailey was secretly glad that the three chairs in the back row were still empty. She slipped into her seat and spread out her story about what had happened to her during the earthquake.

The younger children, and even Justin, had drawn earthquake pictures. His was more like a comic book and he had made an earthquake super hero that looked a lot like himself. Justin had drawn POW!, and BANG! and CRASH! and RUMBLE! in huge jagged letters. Soon after the little kids had had a peek, Justin slid his booklet back into his notebook so only part of it was showing.

"Hey, let me see that," said Fred, pulling it out to see it. "That's awesome, dude. I didn't know you could draw." He handed the comic strip to Noah.

"Double awesome!" said Noah. He tried to smooth his unruly hair, the color of a yellow cat, just like Mr. Will's.

Justin didn't say anything but Bailey could see that he was surprised and pleased.

"He draws comics all the time," said Fern. She gave her brother a hug. "He makes books for us. He didn't think you'd like it though."

Miss Bekka hurried into the room. "I'm glad to see you all again," she said. "Let's begin by having everyone read or show their earthquake stories and pictures."

Daisy, the youngest, started. She had drawn a picture of a stick figure with a wide open mouth and Fern had written down the words.

All the stories were exciting and Bailey soon had a better idea of what everyone had been doing at home or school when the quake happened.

Just when it was her turn to read, she heard a car screech to a stop, then car doors slamming, and the screen door to Keswick Inn burst open. It was Norma Jean and her brothers.

"Hi, everybody. Sorry we're late," said Norma Jean with her big smile.

"We saved seats for you," said Miss Bekka, pointing to the empty chairs in the back.

The door opened again. It was their mother. Flora Fish smiled weakly, as if someone had told her to be nice or she wouldn't get dessert. "I will stay," she announced.

"Of course," said Miss Bekka, warmly. "Welcome." She looked at Fred, who gave Flora Fish his chair, and sat on a footstool near the window.

"Now, where were we?" asked Miss Bekka.

Bailey suddenly didn't want to read her story out loud and was glad that Miss Bekka had forgotten that she was next.

As soon as the session was over, Bailey snapped her fingers for Goldie and they hurried out the door so she wouldn't have to talk to Norma Jean or anyone in the family. She pretended she didn't hear Norma Jean calling her as she walked toward the path to the woods.

19

Diary mysteries

After supper Sugar and Bailey settled into their recliners to watch the news about earthquake damage.

"Wow!" said Bailey. "I had no idea there were so many problems in so many states."

"Some say that they felt it as far north as Canada," said Sugar.

Whenever the reporters talked about Mineral, the epicenter, they showed a video of what happened inside the little grocery store in town. Clerks looked surprised and scared as the security cameras caught the building shaking and cans, boxes, and bottles falling off the shelves. There were other interviews with different shopkeepers, and with the school superintendent. Sugar and Bailey recognized everyone. The television stations showed damage to chimneys, churches, and houses, including the big historic brick one at Cuckoo. Sugar said that you couldn't see a lot of the serious damage because it was inside buildings. Many people couldn't stay in their houses until repairs were made.

"Everybody knows where I live now," said Bailey. Friends in Florida had called or e-mailed to see if she and her grandmother were okay.

"You never knew you'd have such an adventure when you moved here, did you?" asked Sugar.

"Not really," said Bailey. It was still hard for her to figure it all out.

"And now we might have a hurricane on Saturday," said Sugar.

"I know all about those storms," said Bailey, remembering what hurricanes had done in Florida. "They can be worse than quakes."

"Let's hope Hurricane Irene breezes by, but meantime, we'll make sure we have flashlight batteries and extra water. Now, are you ready to look again at our chimney treasures?"

Sugar shooed Shadow off her lap, and set up a small folding table in the back of her library. She covered it with a tablecloth and gently placed the little leather book and the cloth bag on it. Next, she located her magnifying glass, a pen, and a yellow pad.

"Open the book very carefully," she told Bailey, "and let's see what it tells us."

Bailey hesitated for a moment. She didn't want to damage it. She gently opened the cover. On the first page they saw a tiny date written in faded, browned ink: *1848*. Sugar wrote it down on her pad. There were initials at the bottom of the page. *S F*

"I wonder what they mean," said Bailey.

"They might stand for someone's name, or, they might be a code. It depends what else we find inside," said Sugar.

Bailey turned the page. She saw faint handwriting and another date. *D 25*. Bailey tried to make out the words. "I think this might have been a Christmas present," she said. She read: *Father gave me this book. It is the best present ever. He liked the handle I made for his ax. What a feast. Turkey and hare.*

Bailey pulled up a chair and leaned over for a closer look. *D 26 Father said must hang quilt. Safe to stop tonight.*

Bailey said, "What does that mean? There's a drawing on the next page. They are like the ones on the paper we found in the box."

"This is remarkable," said Sugar. "I think the family was involved with the Underground Railroad."

"I heard about that but I don't know much about it," said Bailey. "Didn't people help slaves escape to freedom?"

"Yes, it was very risky for both the runaways to get to safety, and for those people who were helping them."

"Maybe that's why the book was hidden," said Bailey.

"You are probably right," said Sugar. "Go on, please."

Bailey read: *D 27. I heard noises outside after dark. Men went into the barn.* You don't have a barn," said Bailey, puzzled.

"There used to be one just behind the house, but it burned down before I moved back here," said Sugar. "It was very close to the house, so our writer could have heard voices if someone was being hidden in the barn for the night."

Bailey continued: *Dec 31. Father and I rode to Richmond. Stayed near shoemaker. Father bought sugar for Mother and tobacco for Chester. Ordered boots for me.*

On the next page there was a faint drawing of a boy wearing reddish boots and holding a horse. "I wonder if he drew that of himself?" said Bailey.

Sugar held the magnifying glass over the picture. "Looks that way. He's holding a little book, like this, in his hand and he certainly has mentioned boots."

"The next page is blank," Bailey said. "And the next. But look, here's a sketch of a dog, and uh, bear. I think it's a bear." Under the drawing was the date *J 13*, and the word *snow*.

"I thought bears hibernated in the winter," said Bailey.

"Not always," said her grandmother. "In the mountains probably, but not necessarily here, especially if the weather isn't terribly cold. Our writer might have seen or heard about one."

Sugar yawned. "One or two more pages, and then I'm ready to hibernate myself."

"We can look at more tomorrow," said Bailey. She felt tired, too. "C'mon, Goldie." Her dog awkwardly limped to the stairs, but still reached Bailey's bed before she did.

20

Hurricane plans

Bailey hadn't been sleeping well since the earthquake. Worry seeped into her dreams like melting ice cream in a soggy cone. Even though it was still dark, she decided to get up and go downstairs where she found Sugar in the kitchen.

"Yikes!" said Bailey. She jumped as the house shook from an aftershock.

"There was another one about an hour ago," said Sugar. "Shook my bed. I felt like I was on a bumpy road or bouncing on waves."

"I don't like them," said Bailey. She looked for her cats, but they had disappeared and Goldie was under the kitchen table.

"Aftershocks are hard to get used to," said Sugar, "but nothing seems to have fallen." She sipped her coffee and said, "Miss Bekka called. There won't be school today. They're meeting with an attorney about adopting Sparrow."

"Adopting her? When?" asked Bailey.

"As soon as they can set a date in court," said Sugar.

"Will we be able to go?" asked Bailey. "All of us?"

"I hope so. We're part of Sparrow's family," said Sugar. "It's going to be quite a celebration when it's made official."

Bailey smiled. She knew how much the Keswick boys and their foster sister wanted the adoption to happen, just like Noah and Fred had themselves been adopted when they were little. They were babies, though, not like Sparrow, who was seven.

With no school in the morning, Bailey wondered what she and her grandmother would do. She had forgotten about the storm headed their way, but Sugar hadn't.

"With the hurricane possibly here tomorrow night, we need to turn our porch furniture and picnic table upside down so the wind can't blow them away. You can fill buckets and jugs with water and we'll check our flashlights to see if they're working," said Sugar.

"When we lived in Florida, Mom and I used to have a box of hurricane supplies in the garage. We had extra cans of food for ourselves and my cat."

"Good idea. We can pack an emergency box with food we have in the pantry," said Sugar. "I just hope the wind doesn't blow shingles off the roof. I'm glad your dad and Will covered the hole where part of the chimney fell. Let's hope the tarp doesn't blow away."

Bailey filled the empty water jugs and pails she found in the shed. She picked a dozen ripe tomatoes from the garden and popped a handful of sweet red raspberries in her mouth.

It didn't seem right that in less than one week they would have an earthquake, lots of aftershocks, and a hurricane. She wondered if the boy who had written the diary had experienced an earthquake. Did they happen here a long time ago? She'd ask Sugar if they could go to the history museum in Louisa soon to see what they could find out.

21

Henry Box Brown

The hurricane wasn't as bad as they had expected. Leaves blew down, and one large branch fell across the path to Keswick Inn. Bailey and Sugar were relieved that they hadn't even lost their electricity during the storm, but there was a lot of damage closer to the coast, and in Connecticut, Vermont, and New York State.

While they had waited for the storm to pass, Bailey and Sugar took turns reading from the book narrated by runaway slave Henry Box Brown.

"Sugar, listen to this," said Bailey. "He was born in Louisa County near Cuckoo. Isn't that where our earthquake started?"

"Almost exactly at the epicenter," said Sugar. "What else does the book say?"

"Henry was a slave on a plantation near there. He says that Mr. Barret, his master, was pretty kind," said Bailey. She kept reading, then said, "but then the master died when Henry Brown was fifteen and his family was divided up among Mr. Barret's sons. Henry was owned by William. Mmm," said Bailey. She handed the book to Sugar.

MAP OF LOUISA COUNTY

Sugar read, "My mother was separated from her youngest child and it was not till after she had begged most piteously for its restoration, that she was allowed to give it one farewell embrace before she had to let it go forever."

They both sat silently in their chairs listening to rain pelt the windows.

"That must have been so awful for them," Bailey finally said.

"Slavery was terrible," said Sugar. "Do you want to read more?"

"Sure," said Bailey. "I want to know when he got the name 'Box.' Did his parents give him that name when he was born?"

Sugar continued summarizing the story. "Let's see. Henry was sent to Richmond to work at the Barrets' tobacco manufacturing plant. And although William was nice, the people who were in charge of the plant were often cruel to the slaves. For a while things were okay, then a really mean man with a wooden leg was put in charge. Then there was a kinder supervisor, then another cruel one. Henry Brown described him as a 'villain.' He treated the slaves very badly."

When Sugar reached chapter six, Goldie whined and wanted to go out. Sugar glanced at the clock and said, "Oh my, I had no idea that it was getting so late. I'd better get something out for supper."

Just as she stood, the phone rang, "Hello? Yes, Paul, we're doing fine. . . . No. No hurricane damage as far as we know. I think the tarps are keeping water out of the chimney."

Bailey closed the book and left the room to check her e-mail before Sugar might ask her if she wanted to speak with her father.

22

Worries

"You slipped away before I could hand you the phone," said Sugar. She opened the refrigerator to take out leftovers.

Bailey turned her face and said, "I didn't know it was for me."

Sugar looked at her curiously, as if she knew that wasn't true. She slid the leftover tuna-noodle casserole in the microwave then walked across the room and gave Bailey a hug.

"I have the feeling you aren't very happy to have this part of your family living in the neighborhood," Sugar said.

Bailey felt a lump swelling in her throat. She was quiet for a moment then said, "It's just that—" but no words came out. *Just that what?* Bailey wasn't even sure. Sugar's arms were warm and comforting, but how could she tell her grandmother how she felt when she really didn't know?

Okay, she had learned to like Norma Jean after a while several months earlier and they had been e-mailing. And she guessed that her father was all right, but she didn't know him well yet, and wasn't even sure what to do with a father. All her life, until this year, it had just been Bailey and her mother, Molly. Then Molly went to Costa Rica for a year or so, and Bailey had moved in with Sugar. So much had been happening since then. And now, suddenly an earthquake, a hurricane, and . . .

Besides, the Keswicks felt more like family than her own new family. Bailey didn't know how they would all get along. Mostly, she wasn't sure that she liked having them all in the same place at the same time. She liked being alone with the Keswick kids and her other friends. Norma Jean always got a lot of attention because she was friendly and pretty and not at all shy. What would it be like to have her involved all the time?

Then there was her stepmother, Flora. What about her? She didn't seem to like Bailey. Why? Bailey hadn't ever done anything to her. In fact, they didn't even know each other.

"Just that what?" asked Sugar, interrupting Bailey's thoughts.

"I don't know," whispered Bailey.

"When you want to talk, let me know," said Sugar. The microwave beeped.

Bailey hugged back hard, then quickly set the table. The leftovers looked good.

"Your father told me that they plan on moving into Miss Dolly's house this coming week. It's still furnished, which is good because their furniture hasn't arrived yet from Guam. I told him we'd help out. That okay with you?" Sugar settled into her chair.

Bailey wanted to say, "It's not all right that they are moving so close," but instead she nodded and passed the serving dish to her grandmother.

23

More treasures

Sugar and Bailey, wearing their work clothes, loaded the pickup with cleaning supplies, including a vacuum cleaner, brooms, and a pile of old towels. Bailey was still annoyed that her family was moving nearby. She shoved a bucket so hard that the spray bottle of window cleaner fell out.

"I don't know what they'll need," said Sugar, ignoring Bailey's grouchiness.

Bailey and Goldie climbed into the truck. Bailey was glad that Sugar didn't tell her to leave the hound at home. She didn't care if Flora might not like having the dog around. Bailey had already decided she would ask Sugar to take her home if there were any problems. She was almost hoping there were problems so that she could go back to Sugar's.

She had forgotten that it was such a short ride to Miss Dolly's old house just beyond

Keswick Inn. Norma Jean, her long, shiny black hair pulled back with a scarf, rushed out of the house to greet them. She yanked the truck door open and said, "I'm sooo glad you're here! My room is awesome."

As soon as Bailey assisted Goldie to the ground, Norma Jean clapped and said, "C'mon, Goldie. Follow me."

"Wait," said Bailey, but her dog, tail wagging, was trotting next to Norma Jean. Bailey stayed to help Sugar carry supplies.

The house was a little bigger than Sugar's but had brick outside walls instead of wooden siding. The porch floorboards needed to be replaced or repaired and part of the porch railing was missing. The shutters were crooked and paint was chipped. The windows were so grimy that Bailey could barely see her little brothers peering through one. They held up their hands to wave, and she waved back, but it was a little wave—not a big "I'm glad to see you" wave. The faces quickly disappeared.

After she and Sugar lugged the final batch of cleaning materials to the porch, the door swung open. Bailey's dad smiled and reached out to give her a hug. She accepted it without hugging him back. Bailey felt stingy and mean. She didn't like being that way, but didn't know what to do about it. "Hey, Dad," she said finally. The name "Dad" still sounded strange.

"So glad you were able to come today," he said, giving Sugar a peck on the cheek. "The Keswicks said they'd be along soon and together we'll be able to make this house a home. I'm really looking forward to having my entire family together at last." He roughed up Bailey's hair. She quickly smoothed it back and pushed it behind her ears.

"Up here, Bailey," shouted Norma Jean. She was leaning over the railing at the top of the stairs. "Bring window cleaner and paper towels."

Paulie and Sam were sitting on a pile of old bedding that had been pulled off the wooden bed with spindles in Norma Jean's room. "Here, help me," she said as she made up the bed with new sheets and blankets.

Bailey took one end and pulled the sheet tight. "I really like the quilt that was here," said Norma Jean. "It has patterns on it that look like this. I drew them when Mom said to throw the quilt in the pile." She showed Bailey the sketches from her notebook.

"Neat!" said Bailey. "That's just like the drawing in the little diary—"

"What little diary?" asked Norma Jean.

Sam and Paulie jumped up to have a look.

Bailey hadn't planned on telling anyone about what they had found in the attic until she and Sugar had solved the mystery, but now that words had slipped out, she realized that this house might also have pieces of the puzzle in it. Norma Jean might be able to help.

"Sugar and I found it and other stuff when some of our chimney fell apart in the earthquake," said Bailey. "The diary is really old and it had a drawing in it just like this one. Sugar said some people think that quilts were used to help runaway slaves get to safe places through the Underground Railway."

"I know about the Underground Railway," said Norma Jean. "Maybe my quilt was used." She dug in the pile of bedding and pulled it out. "See, there's the design," she said, folding the quilt carefully.

"Let's go see if we have subway quilts on our beds," said Sam.

"The Underground Railroad wasn't a subway train, silly," said Norma Jean, but the boys were already gone.

"Have you been in your attic yet?" asked Bailey.

"No. Dad said we've got to get the house fixed up first before we can explore the attic, root cellar, and old barn," said Norma Jean. She hugged Bailey. "This is so much fun being near you."

"Kids," Flora called, "I hope you're getting your work done. *Bilis.*"

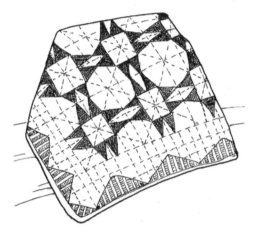

Bailey fluffed the new pillows. "I guess we'd better do the windows," but her eyes traveled back to the design on quilt.

"And don't forget to bring down that filthy old bedding. Your father is going to take it to the dump."

Norma Jean looked at Bailey in alarm. "Oh, no! We've got to hide the quilt. It's too pretty to throw away. I know it needs washing but the stitches are mostly good."

"You could give it to me," said Bailey. "Sugar won't get rid of it. She likes old things."

Paulie and Sam soon returned dragging old quilts that they had pulled off their beds. "Are these special?" asked Paulie.

"Maybe," said Norma Jean. "Bailey is going to take them home to, uh, wash them for us."

"Good," said Sam. "I like this one."

"For now, let's keep them in my closet," said Norma Jean, giving Bailey a knowing look. "We're going to surprise Mom when they are washed."

24

Cleaning continues

With the old quilts out of sight, Norma Jean stood on a stepladder so that she could reach the top of the window glass, and Bailey sprayed and washed the lower section. Norma Jean dropped the old lace curtains to the floor. "I don't know if Mom will want to keep these," she said. "She wants everything new. That's the only thing she likes about moving to the U.S. The malls."

"I thought she wanted to come here," said Bailey. She handed the paper towels to Norma Jean.

"Nuh-uh," said Norma Jean. "I heard them fighting about it one night and—" Before she could finish, Sam interrupted. "Bailey, could you help us make the beds? Mom's going to check them in a minute."

"Sure," said Bailey. She wiped another smudge off the window, then followed the boy.

"You did a pretty good job," she said. "We just need to tuck the sheets under the corner."

"Let the guys show you," said Noah. "We're here to rescue you from the girls."

Sam and Paulie grinned with delight.

Fred and Noah pretended to straighten Sam's bed and quickly neatened Paulie's. "There," said Fred, "what else do you guys want done in your room?"

"Our books and toys aren't here yet," said Sam. "We don't have anything to play with."

"Well, check out this big old box," said Noah. Fred dragged the box they had left in the hall into the bedroom.

The little boys opened the top. "Awesome," said Sam. "Look. Trains, and cars. Dinosaurs. Books."

"We didn't need them anymore," said Noah. "Anything for Bailey's brothers."

Sam and Paulie's eyes were shiny and they had big smiles as they said thanks.

"Now, let's make shelves and put things away," said Fred. With that, Justin, wearing his tool belt, appeared with shelf boards.

"May I help?" asked Paulie.

"Me, too," said Sam.

Within minutes Justin and Fred, with the little boys' help, double-checked the measurements, and began assembling the shelves.

"Are all the windows done?" called Flora. Her voice was filled with annoyance, as if she knew she wouldn't be pleased with their answers.

"We're working on it," said Norma Jean. She motioned for Bailey to follow her to the next room.

25

Aftershock . . . again

Bailey had to admit that by the time they were done, the house looked pretty good. She hadn't spent much time around her stepmother. Bailey preferred to take her lunch outside under the trees rather than to crowd around the kitchen table where Miss Flora was bustling. Soon the other kids had joined Bailey in a hickory grove way beyond the house.

"Our first picnic," said Norma Jean, leaning back against the largest tree. "Boy, it sure is hot in Virginia," she said. Suddenly there was a rumble deep within the ground. Norma Jean grabbed Bailey's leg.

"Just another aftershock," said Bailey. "You'll get used to them." She was surprised at how calm she sounded.

"We didn't have them at the motel," said Sam. "After the quake, I looked in the parking lot, but I didn't see any cracks."

"We had a different kind of earthquake here than in other places of the world," said Fred. "We're going to learn all about it in Earthquake School when Noah and I finish our report." He swatted a mosquito.

"I don't know where I'll be going to school," said Norma Jean. "Mom's upset because the elementary school here was so badly damaged and we might have to be in portables instead of a real building."

"What's wrong with that?" asked Justin. "School is school."

"I dunno," said Norma Jean. "It's just that Mom thinks—" She looked back at the house as if she wanted to see if anyone was headed toward the woods. Then she said, "Maybe we can go to the lake today when we're done."

"Good idea. We've got a beach," said Noah. "I'll ask Dad."

"I'll ask my dad," said Sam. "He always says yes. Mom used to but now—" Paulie put a finger to his mouth to shush Sam.

"Sorry," whispered Sam, "but it's true."

"Gotta go back," said Norma Jean. In the distance they could hear Miss Flora banging on a pan to get their attention.

26

More diary entries

"Mighty interesting old quilts," said Sugar, when she and Bailey returned home after the swim. "Are you sure that Miss Flora didn't want them?"

"Miss Flora was going to throw them away," said Bailey. "Norma Jean said she'd like them."

"Flora might change her mind," said Sugar. "They'll clean up nicely. We'll wash them in the tub and then hang them on a line to dry."

"Just like they did in the Underground Railroad?" asked Bailey.

"We're not sure how true that story is, but yes," said her grandmother.

"Look at this one," said Bailey. "It has the same design as we found in the diary book."

"Let's have a look," said Sugar.

Bailey opened to the page with the sketch.

"Hmm," said Sugar. "Let me get my quilt pattern book."

She opened the book to a page picturing quilt blocks that might have been part of a code for the Underground Railroad.

"See, let's see if this is the North Star design that might have signaled run-aways on the direction they should take," she said. "There was also a song called 'Follow the drinking gourd.'"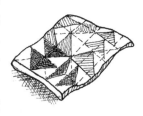

"What did that mean?" asked Bailey. "Were they looking for rivers?"

"The drinking gourd is a reference to the Big Dipper," said Sugar. "Stars were an important part of finding directions before we had the GPS."

Bailey turned another page in the fragile book. *J 26. Shot deer. Roasted with taters. Father going to Pendl.*

The next entry read: *F 15 H. Ander. came late. Voices.*

"I wish he would say more," said Bailey. She turned a few more pages. "Rats. It's faded. Really hard to read. I just see the name *Smith* and *M* something. It might be a *22* or *23*. I can't tell." She handed the diary to Sugar.

"Hmm," said Sugar. "I'm wondering if there's a connection." She picked up the book about

Henry Box Brown and thumbed through the introduction.

Bailey turned her attention to Sugar, who was deep in thought.

"This is a puzzle," said Sugar. "It's giving me a lot to think about." She leaned back in her recliner and the grandfather clock chimed seven. "By the way, do you have homework?"

"Oops," said Bailey. "I almost forgot. I need to find out about earthquakes that happened here a long time ago—if they did. I guess I'd better get busy."

"See what you can find on the Internet, and then we'll set up an appointment at the museum when it's convenient for them. And don't forget to look in my old books for information."

Goldie followed Bailey out of the library and into Sugar's office.

27

Box Brown at the epicenter

Miss Bekka finished working her hair into a thick ponytail as she welcomed the neighborhood children for the morning session. For once, Norma Jean and her brothers were on time. Miss Flora hesitated for a moment in the doorway, then sat on a folding chair in the back of the living room near the fireplace.

"It's probably too soon for reports," Miss Bekka began, but hands went up.

"We have a geological report," said Fred.

"I found out about some of the historic earthquakes," offered Bailey.

Justin shook his head. "Not me. Busy working," he muttered.

"He was helping Mom," said his sister, Fern.

Miss Bekka looked around the room. "Let's start with you, Bailey."

Bailey unfolded papers she had printed out from the Internet.

"This is awesome," she said. "There were a bunch of earthquakes in the 1800s, and get this: There was a bad one recorded in Richmond on August 23, 1802." Trying to pronounce the words carefully, she said, "I read that online in the *Bulletin of the Seismological Society of America,* published in 1913."

"Really! That's the same date as our earthquake," said Sparrow. "Were they all on the same date?"

"You won't believe this! There was another one in Virginia on August 23, 1908," said Bailey, looking at her papers.

"You're kidding," said Noah.

"Amazing," said Fred. "Three on the same date!"

"I know," said Bailey. "And there were other big ones here, too. Sugar has a copy of an old book by geologist George William Featherstonhaugh—she says to pronounce it 'Fanshaw'. He traveled through slave states in 1834 and talked to a lot of people. One guy was Mr. Halliday, who had a plantation in Louisa. Mr. Halliday said he thought his house was at the center of a big earthquake in the summer of 1833 because of the rumblings, but he also thought that the earthquake came from the atmosphere, not the ground."

"That's crazy," said Justin, rolling his eyes. "Everyone knows that's not true. Earthquakes don't come from the sky!"

Miss Bekka said, "It does sound a bit crazy now, but remember that was a long time ago and we now have a lot more scientific information available. Anything else?"

"Two more things," said Bailey, glad that she had spent so much time on her homework. She read: "A man named Mr. T. W. Baker, who was a small boy in Louisa County, remembered the 1833 earthquake. 'He was on his way to school, about eight miles from Louisa County court house, when the earthquake occurred, and it was so violent the fence along the road was visibly shaking.'"

"He must have been really scared," said Norma Jean. "A little kid walking to school by himself when the earthquake happened. I'm going to write a story about that."

"Very interesting material, Bailey," said Miss Bekka. "What are you planning to do as a follow-up?"

"Sugar and I want to locate Mr. Halliday's farm, and I wonder if Henry Box Brown felt the earthquake in Richmond. He would have been there then." The mention of Box Brown had just slipped out.

"Box Brown?" asked Justin. "What kind of name is that?" He snickered and looked around to see if anyone else thought it was funny. Nobody laughed. He rested his face on his arms on top of the table.

Bailey decided that although she and Sugar hadn't figured out why the little diary had a picture of a box and quilt drawings, it was okay to at least mention discovering the book about Box Brown. She hoped Justin wouldn't be rude about it.

"We have a book that he wrote," she began. "Henry Brown was born a slave in Louisa County, near Cuckoo, where our earthquake started. He was sent to Richmond where he earned enough money working in a tobacco warehouse that he could have a house for his wife and children. When his family was sold and taken away to North Carolina, he, with help, shipped himself in a crate to freedom in the North. That's all I know so far."

There was silence in the room. Then Justin raised his head and turned so that he could see Bailey. "Hold on. You mean that the dude built a box and shipped himself away? Really?" Justin sounded genuinely astonished. In fact, Bailey had never seen him so excited about anything she or anyone else had ever said.

Justin rubbed his ear and continued, as if he was thinking out loud, "So, how big was the box? How big was the dude? How long was he in it?" He grabbed his pencil and sketched a box, trying to figure out what it might have been like. "How could he breathe?"

"So how long did it take for him to get shipped there?" interrupted Fred.

Bailey said, "I really don't know anything more. I'll bring it next time so you can see."

"Good idea," said Miss Bekka. "I didn't know about the Box Brown story either. I think we'll take a break now and get some exercise. Everybody outside!"

Norma Jean led the way, with Sparrow wheeling quickly behind her. Bailey stretched and looked back at Miss Flora, who hadn't moved. She seemed to be sewing something in her lap. She glanced briefly at Bailey, then dropped her eyes.

I don't care what she thinks, thought Bailey. *I don't like her either.*

Bailey turned toward the door. To her surprise, Justin was waiting to talk to her.

28

Avoiding Dad

"Do you think Sugar would mind if I came by later to see the book?" Justin asked Bailey. His brown eyes were pleading as if he half expected her to say no.

Bailey didn't think they had any plans after school. "We can ask, but I think it's okay."

"Are there pictures of the box in the book?" Justin asked.

"Just a drawing of it," said Bailey. "That's all I saw so far."

"That dude must have been pretty desperate to escape if he traveled in that box for a more than a few hours," said Justin, thoughtfully. "Was he really born near here?"

"That's what his book says," said Bailey. She was glad that someone was as interested as she was in Box Brown's story.

Justin's attention turned to his sisters. Fern was pushing Martha on a swing while Daisy squatted on the ground, trying to tie her shoe. "I'd better help Daisy," he said.

"I'll tell Sugar you'll be coming over," said Bailey. She had already decided to show Justin what they had found in the attic.

"C'mon, Goldie," said Bailey. "Let's have a little walk before school starts again.

"Wait for me," shouted Norma Jean. Her tan face was flushed from playing tag with her brothers. "Guess what? Dad wants to take you to town with him after school. Just you. Every week each of us has a turn alone with him. We usually go on an errand, like to the hardware store."

Bailey said, "Well, I happen to be busy today. Maybe some other time." She was annoyed that she heard about it from Norma Jean instead of their father, and she knew her voice sounded peeved.

"Okay," said Norma Jean. "Maybe Sam would like to go instead. It's always fun." Norma Jean bent down to kiss Goldie's head. "So what are we doing later, Bailey? Going someplace with Sugar?"

Now Bailey was really annoyed. "It's just Sugar and me and—" She didn't want to mention that Justin was coming over or Norma Jean would show up, too.

"Okay. Never mind. I think *I'll* take your turn with Dad." Norma Jean straightened the headband holding back her long hair. If she was upset with Bailey, she didn't show it. "I'm so glad we moved here," she said, rubbing Goldie's ears. Bailey's hound licked her face.

29

Justin's excitement

Shortly after Earthquake School let out for the day, Justin arrived at Sugar's with his little sisters. "I had to bring them," he said apologetically. "Mom has to work late tonight."

"Not a problem," said Sugar. "We'll have snacks and they can do their homework."

He directed Fern, Martha, and Daisy to the kitchen table and softly told them to work quietly.

"Bailey said you'd like to see the book by Henry Box Brown," said Sugar.

Justin nodded eagerly.

"It's in the library. I'll be there in a moment," said Sugar.

Bailey said, "And we have some other things to show you that we haven't told anyone else about."

Sugar had placed the Box Brown book, the little leather diary, the small wooden box and its contents on the coffee table. Bailey watched Justin's face as he looked at each object.

"What's this stuff?" he asked.

"Have a seat," said Sugar. She let Bailey tell Justin about how they had found things when the chimney collapsed. Bailey then handed Justin the little diary so he could look at it closely.

He turned the pages carefully, reading each entry to himself, his lips silently forming the words.

"There's a drawing of a box," he whispered in awe. "Do you suppose—?"

"We haven't had time to finish studying this diary or Box Brown's own book, but we're wondering if there's a connection," said Sugar.

"Do you think that people who lived here helped him escape?" he asked, his voice cracking with excitement.

"Don't know," said Sugar. "Perhaps you'd like to help with the research."

"Help? Yes, ma'am," Justin said.

Bailey thought that Justin looked like he had won a million dollars. He had been so different recently. When she first met Justin he had teased her, because she was new, and she thought she'd never like him, even a teeny bit. He had been changing, and she realized that he was a lot nicer than she had first thought.

He placed the diary on the table and picked up the horse chestnut. "My grandfather had one of these," he said. "Rubbed it for luck."

He studied the maps and drawings and the little wooden box. His hands ran over the surface as if he were memorizing its size and the wood's grain.

Then he picked up Henry Box Brown's life story. "Amazing!" he exclaimed. "Look at this big dude getting out of that box." He gazed in the air and was quiet for a moment, then mumbled, "Yes. I'll do it."

"Do what?" asked Bailey.

"You'll see," said Justin.

30

Other quakes

Within a few days Sugar was able to locate another copy of *Narrative of the Life of Henry Box Brown* to loan to Justin while she and Bailey continued to read theirs.

"I've never seen him so excited about anything," said Sugar. "Justin's on fire." She leaned back in her recliner in the Book Barn.

"Everybody wants to know more about Box Brown," said Bailey. "They've almost forgotten about their earthquake projects."

"Have you forgotten about yours?" asked Sugar.

"Just a little." Bailey grinned. She rustled through her notebook. "Here's more of the history part. Besides the other Virginia earthquakes I told you about, there was another bad one in 1875 that was felt in North Carolina, Maryland, and Indiana—kinda like our earthquake. A man said, 'It all began with a sound like a rising wind, which increased in violence until the shocks were accompanied by a loud roar. The movement seemed to be from east to west.'"

Bailey paused, "That wasn't exactly what happened at my school, but I wasn't outside."

"It was pretty loud here," said Sugar. "That's a great description, isn't it?"

Bailey looked for papers she had downloaded from the Internet. "Here it is," she said. "It's from the USGS. It says that in the Central Virginia Seismic Zone, since 1774 'people have felt small earthquakes and suffered damage from infrequent larger ones.' Ours was the biggest, though. But listen to this, 'Smaller earthquakes that cause little or no damage are felt each year or two.' Sugar, have you ever felt another earthquake here?"

Sugar said, "There was one reported in the Richmond area in 2003—December, I think, while we were still cleaning up from Hurricane Isabel, but I didn't feel it. Can't say I've noticed an earthquake until this one. I guess I'll be paying more attention when the earth decides to shake, rattle, and roll."

"You're funny," said Bailey. "I'm going to look up the one that happened in 2003." She did a quick search on Sugar's computer and said,

"There were actually two that day—twelve seconds apart—and they felt them as far away as Ohio." She underlined the part about a double event, and added the Ohio Seismic Network to a list in her notebook.

Sugar said, "Shall we read more about Mr. Box Brown before dinner? I've got to confess that I spent time on his book today. What that man, and other slaves, went through touches my heart."

Bailey curled up in her recliner and Sugar said, "This part is particularly awful. Mr. Brown was at work when he learned that his wife, Nancy, and his children had been sold, and were in a prison waiting to be taken the next day to North Carolina. He realized that they would be separated from him forever. He wrote, 'O dear, I thought, shall my wife and children no more greet my sight with their cheerful looks and happy smiles! For far away in the North Carolina swamps are they henceforth to toil beneath the scorching rays of a hot sun . . .'"

Sugar said that Henry Brown found out that if he hurried to a street corner, he could see them go by. One of the wagons carried his eldest child, calling "Father! Father!" Sugar wiped her eyes. "And then he saw his wife's 'precious face,' and he grabbed her hand and told her that they would meet in heaven. He walked four miles holding her hand, and then they were parted."

Bailey had a lump in her throat. She remembered when her mother went off to Costa Rica. Bailey didn't know that she was planning to go away, and she didn't know when she'd see her again. Bailey knew that her mom was happy, and Bailey was living in a good place with Sugar. How terrible for the family of Henry Brown. At least she'd been in touch with her mother. Box Brown's children must have been very frightened when they went away and never heard from him.

Sugar said, "That's enough for now."

"He builds the box next?" asked Bailey.

"We'll find out!" said Sugar.

31

Thinking time

Miss Bekka called while Bailey was washing the dishes.

"That's wonderful news," said Sugar. "I'm marking my calendar right now."

"Adoption day?" asked Bailey.

"Yes, and we're all invited, of course, to the courthouse," said Sugar.

"When?" asked Bailey.

"Next week. They were surprised that it would happen so soon, but the judge had an opening in his calendar."

Bailey thought for a minute, "But what if we're back in school-school?"

"We'll work it out." Sugar dished slices of warm peach cobbler—an old family recipe—into two bowls. "Let's have this on the porch."

"Will Aunt Coco come?" asked Bailey, re-membering the visit from Sparrow's birth aunt, who also was in a wheelchair.

"She'll be there, and all the Keswicks' friends and neighbors are invited," said Sugar. "Afterwards we'll have a grand party."

"We need a special gift for Sparrow," said Bailey.

"Good idea," said Sugar.

Bailey dried her hands on her shorts, then picked up her bowl of cobbler and followed Sugar to the porch. Her grandmother had untangled the porch swing from her rocker and leaned back so she could prop her feet on the railing.

Bailey pulled her purple rocker close to Sugar's so she could do the same. The air was sticky hot. A few fireflies were rising out of the grass. Sugar had marveled that they had been visible all summer this year. The chorus of katydids seemed to swell, filling the otherwise quiet twilight. It was a time of day Bailey really enjoyed. Quiet time with Sugar. "Thinking time," Sugar called it. Sugar seemed to be thinking hard at the moment.

Bailey savored every spoonful of the cobbler, remembering when they drove to an orchard near Charlottesville and picked the peaches. The Keswicks went with them and picked twice as many as Bailey and Sugar did. Miss Bekka said she planned to can most of them so that they could taste the sweetness of summer all winter. Even Sparrow had helped pick fruit from the lowest branches. Sadly, ten quarts had fallen off the pantry shelf during the earthquake, and so had five quarts of pickles and six jars of blackberry jam.

Mr. Will said that he'd fix the shelves so that they would be more earthquake proof just in case the walls shook again.

"What do you think about a scrapbook?" asked Sugar.

"For what?" asked Bailey.

"For Sparrow's adoption."

"That would be a good present," said Bailey. "We could each write a message for her to go in it."

"I like your thinking," said Sugar. "We'll look for one when we go to town this weekend. See if you can pass the word to the other kids about the messages and to keep it a surprise."

Bailey nodded. She hoped Norma Jean wouldn't be a blabbermouth.

32

Justin's request

Justin skidded his rusty bike to a stop and dropped it in the grass near the porch where Sugar and Bailey were sitting. His scruffy brown mutt, Ninja, lay down next to the bike, his tongue hanging out from running to keep up. Goldie whined and thumped her tail in a greeting.

"Miss Sugar," said Justin, tumbling up the steps in excitement, "I have a favor to ask."

"Why sure," said Sugar. "And, if you'd like some homemade cobbler, we have plenty."

"No, thank you, ma'am. I was just wondering—" he hesitated and shuffled his feet like he thought Sugar would say no before he even asked the question.

"Wondering what?" asked Sugar kindly.

"I know you have a basement and I'm wondering if I could work on something there. It's kind of a secret right now."

"Why, sure," said Sugar. "Nobody uses the basement for anything except storing canned goods. Do you need tools or a workbench?"

"Yes, ma'am," he said. "If that would be okay."

"I've got a few—some are rusty, though. I never lock the outside cellar door so feel free to come and go as you need to," said Sugar.

His face beamed. "I'd do it at my house but I really want to keep it a secret, and my sisters would tell."

Sugar thought for a moment. "I know you baby-sit them so if you need to bring them along from time to time Bailey and I might be able to entertain them."

"Thank you," said Justin. "If you ever need help with anything, let me know." He nearly tripped over Ninja, hopped on his bike and sped off with the little brown dog tearing after him.

Bailey was puzzled. *What had come over Justin? What was he up to?*

33

Guessing

"What's going on with Justin?" asked Fred the next morning. Bailey had arrived early at Earthquake School so she could find a good spot to set up the poster she had made. It showed the list of earthquakes in Central Virginia from years gone by. She hesitated, tempted to say something about Justin's mysterious visit, but then stopped herself. Justin had asked them not to tell.

"I don't know," she said, and that was the truth.

"He borrowed tools from Dad and disappeared pretty quickly yesterday evening on his bike," said Noah.

"What did your dad say?" asked Bailey.

"Dad said he didn't know what was going on. He guessed Justin might be fixing something at his house," said Fred, not sounding convinced.

"Maybe that's what he's doing," said Bailey.

"I had the feeling it was something else," said Noah. "We thought you might know."

Bailey was pleased with how her poster looked balanced on the arms of a chair. She walked to the back of the living room and placed her hands on her hips. The lettering was big enough so that the kids, and even Miss Flora, could see from the back row.

"Did you hear?" squealed Sparrow, wheeling into the room. "I'm going to be adopted. My name will be Sparrow Keswick. I will have a forever family!"

Bailey hurried over and gave her a big hug and brushed Sparrow's bangs out of her face.

"You are part of my forever family, too," said Bailey. "Sugar and I'll be there no matter what!"

"Well, little sister, did you do your homework?" Fred asked Sparrow.

"I did. I wrote my story and I read a picture book about Box Brown with my almost mom," she said. "I'm going to give a book report, too."

Bailey thought about the Box Brown story she was reading. That would make a good report, also, but she'd let Sparrow go first with hers.

34

Mysterious pounding

Justin fidgeted throughout the classes, made some notes in a little notebook that he kept in his pocket, and gazed out the window. Miss Bekka tried to get him to focus on school several times. She looked more puzzled than upset with him.

The minute school was over, he ushered his little sisters out the door. Then he hurried them across the back field to the path that led to Sugar's house. Bailey saw them disappear into the woods thick with summer leaves.

"Bailey, can I sleep at your house this weekend?" asked Norma Jean. "I'm sure Mom and Dad will say it's okay."

Bailey glanced at Miss Flora, who was packing up her sewing materials. Her stepmother hadn't even nodded hello when she had arrived with Norma Jean and the boys. Bailey wondered, *Why isn't this woman nicer?*

"I'll tell you tomorrow," said Norma Jean, "unless Dad and I come over later to help with things."

Bailey gathered her books into a pillow case she was using as a temporary book bag, and patted her leg—a signal to Goldie that it was time to go.

"Bye!" yelled Norma Jean. The boys did the same and Bailey waved as she headed for the woods.

The little creek was still bubbling from the rain that fell during the hurricane that had weakened into a tropical storm. Bailey noticed that someone, probably Justin, had placed a log across the narrowest part. She imagined that he helped his sisters cross it. She hopped across the creek and Goldie waded through. Goldie's bandage was very dirty now, but it would be coming off soon.

She saw Sugar sitting at the picnic table with the little girls. Justin and Ninja were nowhere to be seen.

"We were having lemonade," said Sugar, "before we start homework."

Bailey poured herself a glass. She knew better than to ask about Justin in front of his little sisters, even though she could hear pounding coming from the basement.

"I'll do my homework, too," she said.

"What's Justin doing?" asked Fern. "He won't tell us anything."

"It's a surprise for all of us," said Sugar. "Now let me hear you read."

Bailey excused herself so she could go in the house to feed Goldie and get her Box Brown book. As she went inside, the pounding stopped. She was tempted when she came back out to try to peek in the cellar window, but a promise was a promise.

35

Parent problems

Norma Jean passed Bailey a note the next morning. She disguised it by carrying it under a picture she had sketched of Goldie and Clover. After she showed Bailey the picture, the note remained on Bailey's desk. Norma Jean quietly sat in her chair behind her, just in front of Miss Flora.

Bailey studied the note and her cheeks flushed. *I asked about sleeping over. Dad said yes and Mom said no and they got into a big fight. I wasn't supposed to tell you that. Don't say anything.*

Bailey wanted to turn around to ask Norma Jean what was going on, but she knew she shouldn't. *A fight about staying at her house?* She hadn't expected that. She hadn't really cared if Norma Jean slept over, but now she really wanted her to. They had things to talk about.

Miss Bekka asked them to stand for the Pledge, then called on Sparrow to give her book report.

Bailey knew she should be listening, but she was also thinking about Norma Jean and their dad. She decided to write a note back.

Do you want Sugar to call them?

She folded the note and "accidentally" dropped it on the floor where Norma Jean could see it.

36

A walk with Dad

Bailey's dad was waiting outside of Keswick Inn when Earthquake School was over for the day. Bailey waved and was about to run on past him to the Book Barn when he called to her. "Hey, Bailey, would you like to take a walk to the lake together?"

Bailey was surprised . . . very surprised. She was actually pleased that he had personally asked to spend time with *just* her, his oldest daughter, and he didn't seem to care that Miss Flora was watching from the porch.

"You mean just me?" she asked, just to be sure.

"Yes, just you, if it's okay with both you and your grandmother," said her dad. "And Goldie's welcome to come, too." He reached down to pet the dog.

Bailey thought for a moment. She looked back at the porch. Miss Flora stared at her, then quickly turned away to talk to Paulie. Bailey looked at her dad's face. He looked so hopeful that she said, "Let me check with Sugar." She ran to the bookshop to let Sugar know, then whistled for Goldie to follow her on the walk.

"I'm glad for this time to get better acquainted," he said.

Bailey didn't answer. She was still thinking about the somber looks she had seen on the faces of the rest of his family. She thought she had seen a little smile on Norma Jean's, but her stepmother did not look happy at all.

"What a beautiful path," said her father. "It reminds me of where I lived when I was a boy. My brother, Andy, and I played in the woods. We had a fort and fished in a big pond. Mooka Malloo, our cat, always followed us."

"Mooka Malloo's a funny name. I didn't know about your brother or a cat," said Bailey, suddenly curious to know more.

"And a mother and father," he said with a laugh. "Your other grandparents. By the way, they want to meet you when you're ready."

Bailey broke a small branch off a bush and pulled the leaves off. She vaguely remembered Norma Jean mentioning grandparents, but at the time she hadn't thought of them as being *her relatives,* too. She wanted to ask her father about what they were like, but wasn't sure what to say. She didn't know where to begin.

"Do you swim often?" he asked, breaking into her thoughts.

"Some, when we're not busy. The Keswicks have a pontoon boat, and Sugar has a little boat. We like to fish," said Bailey. "I'm getting good."

"That's my girl," said her dad. "I like fishing, too. Maybe we can try our luck together."

"Sure, we have extra poles," said Bailey. She was surprised at how much she wanted to do that. She tossed the stick stripped of its leaves to Goldie to carry.

"The lake's beautiful," said her dad when they stepped on the beach. He kicked off his flip-flops and waded in. "Warm near the shore, but colder out here. Ouch!" he said, as a sunfish nibbled his ankle.

"They don't really hurt," said Bailey. "They just freak out everyone."

"Sure freaked me out," he said, wading deeper. "I guess we don't need to look for sharks or jellyfish in Lake Anna."

"Nope," said Bailey, grinning. She tossed off her shoes and followed him. Suddenly, she felt silly. She kicked water at her dad.

He turned in surprise. "Ah, so it's a water war," he said with a big smile.

Bailey laughed and splashed him with both hands. Her dad scooped water in her direction, thoroughly dousing her hair and clothes.

Goldie, barking from the shore, waded in to rescue Bailey. The dog was soon drenched as the water war continued.

"Truce!" shouted Bailey, wiping water from her eyes and freckled nose.

"Okay," said her dad. "I think we should head back to dry off."

Bailey smiled and picked up her shoes. She decided to walk barefoot up the path rather than coat her new sandals with sand.

"You don't know how I've longed for a moment like this," said her father, with a faraway look in his eyes. "You're just like I hoped you'd be. Smart, fun, caring, and cute like me."

Suddenly Bailey felt sad, confused, and a little angry. *If you really cared, then why didn't you, and your parents, find me before now? Why didn't you tell your wife I'm the oldest? Why didn't Mom talk about you?*

When they reached the Keswicks' yard, her dad was whistling. Bailey didn't say anything.

No one was waiting on the Keswicks' porch. Miss Flora and the children were gone.

37

Missing

Sugar handed Bailey a towel from the clothesline at the inn. "Looks like you had a bit of a splash," she said. "Fun?"

"I guess," said Bailey. "He likes to fish."

"We've got plenty of rods," said Sugar.

"That's what I told him," said Bailey. She decided this was a good time to tell Sugar about Norma Jean's note. "By the way, I think they are having problems. Norma Jean sounds worried because her parents are fighting."

"Did she say what the problems were about?" Sugar's eyebrows furrowed.

"She didn't say, but it might be about me. Her mother didn't want her to sleep at our house but Dad said she could."

Sugar was quiet. "Mmm," she finally said.

"Norma Jean passed me a note. I think she'd like you to talk to her parents," said Bailey. "I mean, I suggested it and she said yes."

"Let me give it some thought," said Sugar. "I'm glad you shared with me. I've been a little concerned about Flora."

"Me, too," said Bailey. "I don't think she likes me at all and she doesn't even know me."

"Mmm. Here's what I think," said Sugar thoughtfully, "and I'm not sure I'm right until I have a chance to talk with them. I think this has been a difficult move for Flora. It's a foreign country. She's originally from the Philippines, but was obviously very happy in her home in Guam with her husband and children. Relocating can be difficult."

Bailey remembered how she felt when she had to move from Florida to live with Sugar. She wasn't happy about that either because she liked her home and had a lot of friends. And then her mother suddenly wanted to go away to Costa Rica for a dream job—something she had always wanted to do—and Bailey found herself alone on an airplane to Virginia where the only person she knew was her grandmother. It was warm in Florida on the day she left, and cold in Virginia when she arrived.

Bailey had felt like crying, but didn't want anyone to know. Maybe Miss Flora, even though she was a grown-up, was having the same feelings. But Miss Flora was a grown-up and weren't grown-ups supposed to act like grown-ups?

She realized that Sugar was talking again. "There may be other issues," said her grandmother. "I'll be glad to have a chat to see if there is anything we can do—and I do mean we."

"We?" asked Bailey.

"Yes, girlfriend. We. We're all family now, as awkward as it may seem at the moment."

Just then the door to the Book Barn banged open and Bailey's dad, still damp from the lake, burst into the room. "Have you seen Flora or the kids?" he asked anxiously. "They're not at the inn, or at our house, and the SUV's gone."

Bailey felt a burn in her heart. Her dad looked so worried.

"Not since school was out, Paul. You're welcome to take my truck to look for them," said Sugar, "Call us when you have news." She tossed the keys to him.

38

This side up

Justin was working in the basement when Bailey, Sugar, and Goldie returned home. Bailey quickly changed out of her damp clothes and brought her Box Brown book out to the porch where she could read more about his escape.

She hoped the phone would ring so they would hear news about her family. As annoying as Norma Jean could be sometimes, there was a lot to like about her. She was always friendly and looking for adventure. They needed to figure out the patterns on the quilts. And Bailey hadn't even had a chance to get to know Norma Jean's brothers, who were Bailey's brothers, too.

She removed the bookmark, placed her feet on the railing, and leaned back.

Box Brown had help from a white man, Samuel A. Smith, who was a shoemaker, and from a free black man, James Caesar Anthony

Smith, who was a dentist. People referred to him as Dr. Smith. They hired John Mattaner, a black carpenter, to build the pine box three feet one-inch long, two feet six inches high and two feet wide. They printed on the side, THIS SIDE UP WITH CARE. The box was not very big, and Henry Brown was five feet eight inches tall and weighed 200 pounds.

How could he possibly have fit in it and stayed in it for twenty-seven hours? Bailey wondered. *How could he eat or sleep or go to the bathroom? What happened if he got the hiccups, burped, or farted, or if his stomach growled? He must have been really desperate for freedom.*

Henry Brown said there were three holes for air and he had a bladder of water for drinking and wetting his face in case he felt faint. He took a tool—a gimlet—to make extra air holes if he needed them.

Henry Brown pretended he needed a few days off from work because of a deliberately hurt finger. Arrangements had already been made in Philadelphia to pick up the crate when he arrived there. He climbed into the box on March 29, 1849, and his friends nailed it shut. As soon as the box reached the Express Office for shipment, someone turned it upside down and he was put in a wagon, taken to a station and "tumbled roughly into the baggage car." The box was placed, again head down, on a steamer at Potomac Creek. He had to remain in this uncomfortable position for one and a half hours, "which from the sufferings I had thus to endure, seemed like an age to me, but I was forgetting the battle of liberty and I was resolved to conquer or die."

Box Brown did a lot of praying. Eventually two men turned the box on its side so they could sit on it, and after wondering what was in it, decided it was mail. "I too thought it was mail, but not such a mail as he supposed it to be," wrote Henry Brown.

The box arrived in Washington, where it was removed from the steamer and placed in a wagon, and then taken to the train station. Men dropped it and Henry feared his neck had snapped. Eventually the box was placed in the baggage car, right side up. After traveling 350 miles, the box arrived in Philadelphia and was delivered to the abolitionists.

Box Brown wrote: "I heard a man say, 'Let us rap upon the box and see if he is alive.'" Everyone was overjoyed when he answered and they opened the box. "I rose a freeman, but I was too weak . . . to be able to stand," and so he fainted. When he recovered, he sang a hymn of thanksgiving from Psalm 40, and eventually was helped by antislavery friends to get farther north, to Massachusetts, where he was supposed to be safer.

"This is so amazing," Bailey said. "I can't wait to tell everybody."

Bailey started to read a poem that Box Brown wrote about his experience when she heard Justin close the cellar doors. He stopped by the porch before he went home. "Almost done," he said. "One more day." He hopped on his rusty bike and peddled off, with Ninja running to catch up.

The phone still hadn't rung when Sugar said supper would be ready as soon as Bailey set the table. There was still no call when Bailey and Goldie walked up the stairs and past the room that Norma Jean had stayed in when she had visited during late winter.

I sure hope everyone's okay, thought Bailey.

39

Still no word

Sugar was humming in the kitchen when Bailey padded downstairs for breakfast.

"Good news," she said, pouring juice for Bailey.

"Did he call?" Bailey was still having trouble calling Paul Fish "Dad."

"Not yet, but it's early. According to a recorded message we got this morning, you'll be going back to middle school next week—at least every other day until they have enough portable classrooms set up for the high school students to use," said Sugar. "And best of all, school won't conflict with the adoption day."

"What happens at an adoption? Do we say anything?" asked Bailey, slicing two peaches.

"Probably not. I've already written a letter of support, telling officials that the Keswicks are a wonderful family."

"That will be so great," said Bailey.

"And also, I had a long e-mail from your mom this morning," said Sugar. "You'll want to read it."

"What did she say?" asked Bailey, spreading homemade blackberry jam on her toast.

"It was just chatty. She asked how you and your dad are getting along," said Sugar.

"What did you tell her?"

"I thought you'd like to answer it," said Sugar.

Bailey didn't know what to say to her mom right now. She decided to read her e-mail later.

Bailey looked at the kitchen clock, one that Sugar had bought at a yard sale. It always ran fast so Bailey was never quite sure of the time. Sugar said if it was fast they'd get to places early, which was better than running slow and being late.

Bailey washed the dishes and said, "Gotta go." She grabbed her homework and books, called for Goldie and off they dashed through the woods to Keswick Inn.

Bailey slid into her chair in time for the Pledge. There were three empty chairs behind her.

Miss Bekka said, "As some of you may have heard, your regular schools will start again next week on a special schedule. We'll continue to have Earthquake School here on the days you don't go there, so you can come over here to do your homework or sit in on our lessons."

A car door slammed in the yard, and then another. Norma Jean and her brothers rushed through the front door and hurried to their seats. Norma Jean wasn't smiling and their mother wasn't with them.

40

Family matters

Bailey thought about slipping a note to Norma Jean, but decided to wait until recess to ask what was going on.

Fern and her sisters passed around the stories they had written and illustrated about the earthquake and nobody seemed to mind that Martha had drawn tigers and monkeys next to the picture of her house. She said the earthquake sounded like a tiger's roar.

Bailey reported on what she had been reading about Box Brown and the box itself. Justin, who had been looking out the window, interrupted to described the box in great detail.

"Why do you think Henry Brown would take the risk of escaping in a box?" asked Miss Bekka.

"He wanted his freedom," said Fred.

"Didn't a lot of slaves want their freedom?" she asked.

"Yes," said Justin "but he was very upset about the people he had to work for and especially that they sold his wife and children."

"Family's very important, isn't it?" said Miss Bekka. "Did Mr. Brown ever see his wife and children again?"

"No," said Justin. "I read the whole book. He traveled around New England talking about slavery and then, when the law changed, and he wasn't even safe in the North, he sailed to England. He had escaped, but he wasn't legally free."

"Thank you," said Miss Bekka, clearly impressed with Justin's research. His face flushed with embarrassment and he doodled on his math homework.

Family's important. Bailey thought about what Miss Bekka said and about Box Brown. She remembered how close Henry had been to his mother when he was a boy on the plantation near Mineral. His mother had told him, as she pointed to forest trees that had lost their leaves in the fall, that children of slaves are torn from their parents just like the wind blows leaves off the trees.

Bailey thought about how much Henry Brown loved his wife, Nancy, and had tried to provide a home for her and his children and how he had walked for four miles holding her hand when she was being taken away to North Carolina.

She thought about her own new family. What would Box Brown have thought if he learned that he had family he didn't know about? *Family's important.* He probably would have been really happy.

She then thought about her father moving halfway around the world in order to bring his children together. Suddenly she was very proud. Even if she hadn't known her father for most of her life, she realized that he really did care about her and the rest of the past didn't matter.

She looked back at Norma Jean's sad face and smiled at her.

41

Threat

"What's going on?" Bailey asked her sister during recess. Norma Jean and the boys had not rushed outside with the rest of the kids.

"I'm not supposed to talk about it," said Norma Jean. "At least, not yet." She pulled her straight black hair behind her head and fastened it with a green clip.

"I'll tell you," said Paulie. "Mom wants to go home to Guam. We went back to the motel and then Dad found us."

"Shh," said Norma Jean.

"Mom was crying and so was I, but I want to stay here," said Sam.

"Why doesn't she like it?" asked Bailey. "You haven't been here very long."

"Listen," said Norma Jean. She moved close to Bailey so she could whisper in her ear. "Mom's afraid Dad will like you best because you're the oldest instead of me."

"That's silly," said Bailey.

"I know," said Norma Jean, "but she didn't know much about you until last year, and now we moved to be near you. Besides, she doesn't know where she'll find the kind of foods she liked to eat back home, like sweet mangoes, banana lumpia, and halo-halo from the little restaurant near us."

"And who will be her friend now if she's so grumpy?" said Paulie.

"She didn't used to be so grumpy," said Sam. "She used to smile and sing."

Bailey looked at their gloomy faces. "Sugar will think of something," she said. "It will all work out."

Family matters.

"I'm glad you're are here," Bailey said, "and anytime you want to pet Goldie or take her for a walk, go ahead. You can hold my cats, too, and I'd like you to come to my house. We have tons of books."

"If Mom ever lets us," muttered Norma Jean.

42

Justin's surprise

Mr. Will and Justin arrived early the next morning and disappeared into Sugar's basement. Bailey wanted to see what they were up to, but Sugar told her to hurry along to school. Goldie dashed ahead of her through the woods. Bailey was happy that the dog was no longer limping. Norma Jean and the boys were already in their seats, waiting quietly for class to start. Miss Bekka looked at her watch and said, "I guess we'll begin without Justin."

As soon as the Pledge was finished, a truck pulled up in the driveway and Justin and Mr. Will came to the door. "Give us a hand," Mr. Will said to Noah and Fred. The four of them struggled through the door with a large wooden container, which they set down at the front of the classroom.

Miss Bekka beamed. "Can anyone tell me what this is?"

Some of the younger children shouted that it was a dog house or a doll house. Bailey read: THIS SIDE UP WITH CARE. She looked at Justin's face and realized what he had been doing in the basement for several days.

"It's like the box that Henry Brown made," she said.

Justin patted the box. "It's the same size exactly. I followed the dimensions. But it is different. The original box was nailed shut and

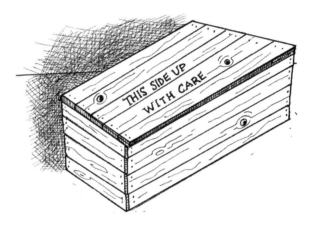

there were straps around it to keep it closed. I made a sliding door and put a hook inside so he could fasten himself in and get out if he wanted to—if nobody was around. That way he could stretch his legs. The real box was also lined with canvas, but I didn't have any."

"Can I try it?" asked Paulie.

"You bet. Everyone can see what it's like," said Justin, looking at Miss Bekka to make sure it was all right.

Mr. Will said that because he was taller than Henry Box Brown, he should go first to show everyone how cramped a grown man would be in a wooden crate this size. Justin slid open the panel and all the kids crowded around to watch Mr. Will. He bent down, trying to curl up with his hands around his knees. "Yikes! This wouldn't be comfortable for very long," he said. "I think five minutes is all I could manage."

"Yeah, but you weren't desperate for freedom," said Noah.

Everyone, including Miss Bekka, took turns trying out the crate.

"Did he have food or anything to drink?" asked Sparrow. "I would like chocolate milk if I were going to be in a box."

"No chocolate milk," said Justin, but he did take water in a bladder—a container." Justin then climbed into the box, leaving the sliding door open. "Now turn it upside down," he said, "and you'll see what it was like when he had to ride that way for twenty-seven hours."

Fred said, "That position looks really uncomfortable."

"It is," said Justin. "Turn me back."

"What happened when Box Brown reached Philadelphia?" asked Miss Bekka.

Justin said that the book had a picture of men opening the crate and Henry Brown coming out. Miss Bekka helped him out of the box so he could show everyone the illustration.

The Resurrection of Henry Box Brown at Philadelphia. *Lithograph, copyright January 10,1850. Courtesy of the Library of Congress.*

"I hope you'll share this project with your class at middle school, Justin. This is very impressive work," said Miss Bekka.

Justin looked especially pleased when Noah said, "Great job, dude."

"We'll give you a hand taking it to your school," said Mr. Will.

"Maybe," said Justin. His face clouded and Bailey heard him mumble something about not knowing if anyone else would like it.

Bailey said, "Of course, they will!"

Justin looked at her, surprised. "Maybe," he said again.

43

More questions

Paul Fish was waiting outside when school was out for the day. Bailey watched her brothers run over to hug him. He looked at her with a big smile, but his eyes appeared worried. His face was happy and sad, like it seemed in the one picture she had of the two of them from when she was a baby. She wondered if he remembered that picture, which Sugar had given her from her baby album.

Norma Jean asked, "Where's Mom? She didn't come to school today."

"Resting," said their dad.

"Where?" asked Norma Jean.

"We'll talk about it later, kiddo," he said, pulling Norma Jean close to him. Bailey wished she hadn't held back the last time her dad had tried to hug her. She wondered what would happen if she moved close enough for her father to pull her under his other arm. Before she could try, he led Norma Jean and the boys to his car, then turned and waved at Bailey.

Bailey watched them drive off, then walked with Goldie over to the Book Barn. Sugar wasn't there and she hadn't left a note, so Bailey figured she must be at home.

The earth rumbled again while she jogged through the woods. She was surprised that she was no longer as frightened by the aftershocks. Sometimes they rattled the windows and pictures moved on the walls, but they were not as fierce as the earthquake. Instead, they made for something to write to her friends about.

Sugar had left a plate of peanut butter cookies and a note for her on the kitchen table. *I'm on a mission to see what I can do for Flora,* said the note. *Get your homework done and perhaps we'll have time to go fishing later.*

Bailey ate two cookies, and fed Goldie and the cats. She wondered what Sugar could possibly say or do to make things better.

She finished her homework, then opened the little diary.

Mar 30. Another visitor at night. Gone in morning. Old Ben said shipment on its way. Hopes he gets there.

Shipment? He? Bailey wondered if the diary writer was talking about Box Brown. There were enough clues that made it seem like it could be the same story. *That would be so cool,* she thought.

Bailey turned more pages. "All I see is *A 14* and the word *success*. I wonder what this means," she said softly.

She heard the screen door open. "Either my only best granddaughter is home, or the cats ate my cookies," Sugar called from the kitchen.

"In here," said Bailey, "in the library. I have something to show you."

Sugar was very interested in the diary entry and also the one they read from the next day that mentioned another planned trip to Richmond for shoes.

"They sure buy a lot of shoes," said Bailey.

"That might be code," said her grandmother, "or, if this family was really part of the Underground Railroad, perhaps they were getting shoes to give to the escaped slaves to protect their feet when they reached colder places."

"Do you think that's really true?" asked Bailey.

"The problem is that we may never find out. Without proof, we won't know for sure."

"What kind of proof?" asked Bailey.

"We'd need to know the name of the person writing the diary, and his or her family name and we'd have to see what we could find out about them. Did they live here when the diary was written, or were they living somewhere else? There's a lot we don't know."

"We can pretend, though," said Bailey. "It's still a good story."

"And some day we may find proof about this diary," said Sugar.

Bailey turned more pages. "I see one other entry," she said. "It has to do with groceries. It's a list and a a few sketches: flour, sugar, tea and other things like needles and thread. That's it." She was disappointed. Then she saw a faint word. She held it to the light. It looked like the word "earthquake."

Sugar said, "Time for fishing. I think we'll have some company in the boat."

44

Fishing with family

Bailey was astonished to see her father and Paulie waiting for them at the boat ramp. Her little brother was wearing a life vest and holding a small fishing pole.

"The rest wanted to come," said her dad, "but I know Sugar's boat can safely hold only four, so we'll take turns."

Bailey slipped into her life jacket and pushed her hair behind her ears.

"I can bait my own hook," said Paulie.

"Well, you can bait mine, too," said Bailey, laughing.

"Nuh-uh, girls have to do their own," said the boy. He took a night crawler out of the small white carton they had purchased at the marina and slipped a worm on the hook.

"We need to get out in the lake before you cast your line," said Sugar. "No fishing in the parking lot."

Soon after the boat was launched, Sugar yanked the cord for the engine and it sputtered, then started.

The lake was quiet. Sugar aimed the boat into a cove and told Paulie to watch for beaver huts. "The crappies like to hide out there," she said.

When they saw a pile of logs and sticks by the shore that beavers had made into a home, she stopped the engine and let the boat drift close to it. Little bugs skittered on the surface and a turtle eyed them and slid off a log into the water without making a splash.

Paulie cast expertly in the direction of the beaver hut while Bailey selected a worm for her hook. She saw her father smile and she grinned back. She cast off the other side of the boat so she wouldn't tangle her line with Paulie's.

Bailey heard her father's bobber hit the water and Sugar whisper that she would just watch the fun rather than fish today.

"I got one!" yelled Paulie, excitedly. He yanked and reeled, but there was nothing on his line—and the worm was gone.

Bailey studied the dark water, hoping to feel the tug of even a little sunfish, but there were no bites.

"I hear the lake was pretty wild during the earthquake," said her dad.

"Friends out in their boat that day said that there were waves, bubbles from the bottom, and fish jumping. They heard the roar of the generators when the power plant shut down," said Sugar.

"Must have been scary," Paul Fish said.

"Got one!" shouted Paulie, reeling fast.

A little sunfish squirmed on the end of his hook.

"Let me take a picture, kiddo, and then we'll toss it back."

Paulie posed proudly with a fish not much bigger than Bailey's hand. "I want Bailey in the picture, too," he said. Bailey squeezed onto the seat next to him and saw his big grin.

His was the only fish anyone caught. Sugar told them that the fishing was much better early in the morning, and that they'd try again another day.

"Maybe we can all go out in the Keswicks' pontoon boat," said their dad. "I know Sam and Norma Jean would like to join us."

After they had hauled the boat out of the water, Bailey moved close to her father while he rinsed off his flip-flops at the edge of the ramp. He didn't seem to notice that she was near enough for a hug, so she returned to the pickup and climbed in the back seat with Paulie.

To Bailey's surprise, Miss Flora was waiting for them in Sugar's yard. "Do you have Sammy with you?" she called out frantically to them.

"Just Paul . . . and Bailey," their dad responded.

"I have no idea where he went," she said. Bailey could see that she had been crying. "You've got to find him!"

"We'll all look," said Sugar.

"He wanted to go fishing with you," said Miss Flora, "but you took *her* instead."

"It's certainly not Bailey's fault," said Paul Fish, with an edge to his voice. Bailey heard him mutter, "You were supposed to be watching him, Flora."

"We can put things away later," said Sugar. "Let's find Sam first."

"He's so little and he doesn't know where we are," said Miss Flora. "It's not like home."

"We'll find him," said Sugar. "He'll be fine."

Bailey didn't wait to hear Miss Flora's answer. It wasn't fair that her stepmother was blaming her because she couldn't find Sam.

Her dad was right. Miss Flora should have been paying better attention. Still, he was just a little boy and it would be scary to be lost in an unfamiliar place.

Bailey ran hard through the woods to Keswick Inn, calling his name. She stopped twice to listen for an answer, but heard no response. "Help me find him, Goldie," she said. "You're a hunting dog. Hunt for Sammy."

When they reached the orchard behind the inn, Bailey heard Norma Jean shouting for her brother from down near the Keswicks' beach. Miss Bekka's thick blond hair was coming loose from its braid as she rushed through the holly woods surrounding the orchard.

"Noah, Fred, and Will have gone to Miss Dolly's house to search there. I'm glad you're back to help," Miss Bekka said.

Bailey looked through the Book Barn, and then the big barn, checking the stalls and behind hay bales. She figured Miss Bekka had already been there, but she might have overlooked a clue. There was no sign of Sam. He wasn't just any kid they were looking for. *Sam's my little brother. We have to find him before it gets dark.*

"C'mon, Goldie. Use your nose," said Bailey.

Goldie whined and looked at her.

"Find Sammy." Bailey knew that Goldie didn't really know who Sammy was, but it wouldn't hurt to tell her to look. Dogs could be really smart sometimes.

In the distance she could now hear Sugar, her father, and Paulie also shouting and Norma Jean answering that she hadn't seen Sam. How worried her sister must be!

Bailey sat on the steps of Keswick Inn. She wondered where she should search next. Goldie whined. "You're a good girl. I know you'd like to help." Bailey rubbed her ears. Goldie whined again and tugged on her sleeve. "I know it's supper time," said Bailey. "Maybe we can find one of Clover's biscuits in the kitchen."

She stood up and Goldie bounded up the steps and gave a low bark.

"I'm coming," said Bailey. She expected the dog to wait by the door so they could go inside, but instead Goldie went over to the box that Justin had made. She scratched on it.

"Don't do that," said Bailey. "Justin will be mad." Goldie barked and scratched harder.

"There's nothing in there," said Bailey. "Or is there?" She tried to figure out how it opened, then found the sliding door that latched from the inside so that Box Brown could keep it from being opened accidentally. *That's strange,* she thought. *I wonder.* She knocked on the wall. "Sam? Are you in there? Sammy?"

Goldie continued to whine and scratch.

"Sammy, knock on the box if you can hear me," said Bailey. She heard a faint tapping.

"Sammy, listen, it's me, your big sister, Bailey. Can you open the latch? Tap if you can do it." She couldn't hear tapping but a little voice said, "It's dark."

Bailey tried to remember what it was like inside the box. She thought, then said, "Find the latch and unhook it and I'll help you out."

"I can't," said the voice and she could hear sobbing.

"Goldie, go find someone," said Bailey. "Go find anybody." The hound looked at her, then trotted down the steps and across the yard.

"Sammy, keep trying. Everything's going to be okay. Just move your hand on the hook." The crying stopped. "See if you can pop it out," Bailey said loudly.

Suddenly, Bailey heard a clicking sound. She tugged on the sliding panel again and this time it opened and out rolled Sammy. His cheeks were streaked with tears, but he gave Bailey a big smile as he climbed into her arms.

She smelled his sweaty hair, and hugged him tightly.

"I found him," she shouted. "Let's ring the dinner bell, Sam, to let everyone know."

"Where was he?" Miss Flora demanded, grabbing Sam from Bailey's arms.

"I was in the box," he said. "I fell asleep."

"That's a dangerous thing to have around children," said his mother to Miss Bekka.

Bailey stood back, wondering why her stepmother never had anything nice to say. She felt Norma Jean's arm slip around her waist and then big hands on her shoulders. At first she thought they were Sugar's, but soon realized that the hands were her father's.

"I'm proud of Bailey for locating Sam and helping him get out. You really used your head, kiddo!" he said loudly.

Bailey's face flushed with pride. Her father had called her "kiddo," just like he said to the others. Impulsively, Bailey turned around and hugged him. He held her close.

"Flora," he said without letting Bailey go, "we are a family. All of us. And there is enough love to go around. Just because Bailey is my first daughter, doesn't mean I love you, Norma Jean, Paulie, or Sam any less. In fact, I love you all even more."

He pulled Norma Jean into the hug with Bailey. Paulie ran over and squirmed in and Sam told his mother that he wanted down. Soon Bailey felt his little body as he grabbed her legs.

"You're welcome to join us," Paul Fish added, but Flora didn't move. She covered her face for a moment, then wiped her eyes.

"I'm sorry," said Miss Flora, with a shaky voice. Bailey couldn't tell if she meant it or what she was sorry about.

Sugar said softly, "Flora, you've had a hard day. How about a glass of sweet tea?

Miss Flora whispered, "Thank you."

45

Adoption Day

The sky was overcast when Bailey woke up. Norma Jean was sleeping on a cot in her room, but sat up as soon as she heard Bailey's feet hit the floor. They had laid out their clothes the night before so it didn't take long to dress.

"I've never been to an adoption," said Norma Jean.

"Me, neither," said Bailey. "Sugar says it won't take very long so we don't want to be late."

They heard a rumble. "Do you think that's thunder?" asked Norma Jean, brushing her shiny hair.

"Might be another aftershock," said Bailey, looking around. "Are you ready to start school?"

"I wish I was going to your school, not elementary," said Norma Jean.

"Maybe you'll get promoted to middle school," said Bailey. She sort of hoped that would happen. It would be fun to ride the bus together.

Bailey ran a brush through her hair, then slipped on her good sandals—her new ones for starting middle school. They were the ones she was wearing when the earthquake happened.

They found Sugar in the kitchen mixing milk and eggs for scrambling. Bailey set the table and Norma Jean toasted slices of homemade oatmeal bread.

"Sleep okay?" asked Sugar. "I heard you two talking when I went to bed."

"I guess it was late," said Norma Jean happily. "I love being here again."

"We'll have to eat quickly," said Sugar, "so we can get to the courthouse early."

It was about a half hour's drive from the lake to the domed brick courthouse in Louisa. Scaffolding was around the top and workers were on the roof. Sugar found a parking place down the block and they quickly walked to the building and up the steps.

There was a small crowd in the hall waiting for the doors to open. It included Fred and Noah, Mr. Will, Miss Bekka and, of course, Sparrow, who was quietly sitting in her chair, her hands gripping the sides. Aunt Coco was beaming from her wheelchair that was parked near Sparrow's. The elevator opened and out stepped Paul Fish, Flora, and the boys, followed by a social worker, the guardian ad litem, who had been appointed to represent Sparrow, and the Keswicks' family attorney, a tall, balding friendly man with glasses. He carried a bulging leather briefcase. The attorney spoke with the Keswicks, then bent down and whispered something to Sparrow. Bailey saw Sparrow nod and answer.

Mr. Will pulled open the door to the courtroom and everyone found seats on pew-like benches in the back behind the attorneys' chairs. Bailey looked around at the blue woodwork, the color of Sugar's favorite teapot, and the four tall windows behind the judge's bench. She heard the doors open again, and the Rudd family came in and sat behind them.

"All rise," said a man wearing a uniform, and they stood as the judge, in a long black robe,

entered from a side door. He smiled at the Keswicks and told everyone to have a seat.

Bailey's mind wandered until the judge said that the adoption of Sparrow was on the docket. He invited the Keswicks and Sparrow to step to the rail. When the family stood up, Bailey expected Fred or Noah to release the brake on the wheelchair so that Sparrow, with a yellow ribbon in her hair, could wheel herself forward. Instead, Noah locked the brake. Sparrow used her arms to push herself up, and took several wobbly steps so that she was standing in front of the judge. Bailey blinked back tears. She had never seen Sparrow stand alone. Yet, here was Sparrow walking. She was walking to her adoption.

Mr. Will put his arm around the little girl, and the judge began. He asked if Sparrow understood what was happening. Sparrow said loudly so that everyone could hear, "I'm being adopted and this is my forever family."

Within a few minutes, it was official and Paul Fish and Aunt Coco took pictures.

Then, still standing, Sparrow turned, and said with grin, "Now I'm Sparrow Keswick. Forever!"

Bailey's hands hurt from clapping as Mr. Will lifted Sparrow back into her chair, where she would have to stay for a few more months until her hips were completely healed. Fred rumpled her hair and Noah planted a kiss on her cheek.

When they returned to the hallway, Sparrow said, "Wait, I made something for everyone." She reached into a pocket attached to her chair, and removed paper hearts that she had cut out. On each she had written either "Love," "I love you, or, "I love my family."

Sparrow said, "Here. I made one for everyone." She even had a big one for Miss Flora. As the woman held it in her hand, she stared, and then she smiled—a big, happy smile like Norma Jean's. She bent down and kissed Sparrow on her head.

Then, to Bailey's surprise, Miss Flora walked over to Bailey and without a word, took her hand, and pressed the paper heart in her palm. Bailey could see tears in the woman's eyes.

46

New beginning

"That was sure special," said Sugar. "I got a kick out of how many times during the party that Sparrow referred to Bekka and Will as Mom, and Dad, and the boys as her real brothers."

"They were just as happy," said Bailey. "She calls me her 'almost sister.' She sure liked her scrapbook. Now she can add pictures from the adoption and party to it."

They drove home past Bailey's middle school, and the closed high school, which was surrounded by yellow tape to keep people away.

"Do you think you'll do a report on Box Brown for middle school?" asked Sugar.

"I hope so," said Bailey, "if Mr. Patton will let me." It was going to be strange to go back to a real classroom every other day instead of Earthquake School in the Keswicks' living room. Bailey knew she'd miss seeing all the kids, especially her family, every day.

She looked at the paper heart that Miss Flora had handed her. She would have to think of something to give her in return. Maybe she could bake peanut butter cookies to take to their new house. It still felt odd to have a new "family" but she was going to try to be nicer about everything.

Sugar didn't turn down the road to the lake. "Where are we going?" asked Bailey.

"It's a beautiful day. Let's go pick more peaches while they're still in season. What do you think?"

"Deal," said Bailey, happy to be off on another adventure with her grandmother. She thought for a moment, then said. "How about picking an extra basket for Miss Flora? Norma Jean said she misses having fresh fruit. Maybe we could show her how to make your grandmother's special cobbler."

Sugar reached over and patted Bailey's shoulder. "That's my girl," she said with a big smile. "Deal."

Discussion questions

1. Give examples of ways Sugar turns bad situations into good. What is it about her personality that she does that so often?

2. Why is Bailey not so happy that her father and his family are moving nearby?

3. Do Paulie, Sam, and Norma Jean have anything in common with Bailey other than their father? How are they different from Bailey?

4. Flora says, "bilis," the word for hurry in the language of the her native land, the Philippines. Do you know children who speak a language at home that is not English? Have they ever spoken that language in front of you with others? Did you ever feel left out?

5. What specific events lead Bailey to think Flora does not like her?

6. Bailey, Justin, and his sisters attend "homeschool" with the Keswicks while their

schools are closed from earthquake damage. How is homeschool different from public school? How is it the same? What do you think you would like or dislike about homeschooling?

7. Henry Brown built a box and shipped himself to freedom. Why did he need to do that? Why would he take the risk? What happened to his family? What do you think would be hardest about being in a box for so long?

8. Why do you think Justin is so interested in the Box Brown story? Are there, or were there, ever situations or people Justin would have liked to escape?

9. Is there anything Bailey would like to escape or run away from? Did you ever feel like running away? Write about it.

10. Sometimes parents in families with more than one child plan "alone" time for each child with each parent. Does your family do this? Most children love it. Why does Bailey turn down going to town alone with her dad?

11. For Sparrow's adoption day Bailey and Sugar decide to give her a scrapbook. Why is this a good gift? What would you give her?

12. Why do you think Flora and Paul fight about Norma Jean wanting to sleep over at Bailey's house?

13. When Bailey's dad says, "You are the daughter I hoped you would be," why does Bailey feel angry and sad?

14. How is Bailey able to understand what Flora might be feeling now that Flora is so far from her home in Guam?

15. Where is Guam? How big is it? How long would it take to get there from where Bailey lives? Name three ways Guam is different from Virginia.

16. What did you think was going to happen when Flora left with the three children and Paul was frantic to find them? Write down three other things that might have happened to them, and then write a longer version of one of those ideas. Let your imagination go crazy.

17. Why is it important to the story that Bailey finds Sam? Why do you think he hid where he did?

18. What does Miss Flora give Bailey at Sparrow's adoption? What is Bailey thinking about giving Flora in return?

19. What would Sugar say makes a family a family? What kind of families can you think of?

Web sites

http://www.geol.vt.edu/outreach/vtso/

http://.neic.usgs.gov/

http://earthquake.usgs.gov

http://docsouth.unc.edu/neh/brownbox/ brownbox.html (text of book)

http://albertis-window.blogspot.com/2010/09/ henry-box-brown (moving panorama)

http://www.virginiamemory.com/ online_classroom/lesson_plans/ henry_box_brown_escapes_slavery

To read Box Brown's narrative on-line: http:// docsouth.unc.edu/neh/boxbrown/ boxbrown.html

http://www.menare.org/ (to learn more about the Underground Railroad)

(Sites are available as of press time. Author and publisher have no control over material on these sites or links to other Web sites.)

From Sugar's bookshelves

A Picture of Freedom: The Diary of Clotee, a Slave Girl, Patricia C. McKissack

Bulletin of the Seismological Society of America, 1913

A Cord of Three Strands, Holly Moulder

Eyes of the Calusa, Holly Moulder

Harriet Tubman: Conductor on the Underground Railroad, Ann Petry

Henry's Freedom Box: A True Story from the Underground Railroad, Ellen Levine and Kadir Nelson

Narrative of the Life of Henry Box Brown, written by himself

The Young and Field Literary Readers, Book four, Ella Flagg Young and Walter Taylor Field

The Unboxing of Henry Brown, Jeffrey Ruggles

To Be a Slave, Julius Lester

Mineral's earthquake

On August, 23, 2011, a 5.8 magnitude earthquake with the epicenter near Mineral rattled Central Virginia and the East Coast. The shallow earthquake, about eight kilometers deep, happened on a fault of a type common to this part of the country, said Martin C. Chapman, PhD, associate research professor in the Department of Geosciences, at Virginia Tech, and also the director of the Virginia Tech Seismological Observatory (VTSO). He said the ground shook hard in the epicenter area, which is part of the Central Virginia Seismic Zone, for about two and a half seconds. Researchers will be studying this earthquake and its aftershocks for a long time. The August, 23, 2011, earthquake was the largest to have occurred in the central Virginia zone in recent time. The second largest was in 1875 with magnitude estimated at between 4.5 and 5.0, Dr. Chapman said.

Henry Box Brown

Henry Box Brown was born in 1815 on a plantation called The Hermitage at almost the exact location of Mineral's 2011 earthquake. Much of his story is relayed when Bailey, Sugar, and Justin read his narrative. Historians believe

 that Brown told his story to people who wrote it down for him. Several editions were printed.

He became a spokesperson for the Abolition movement that was trying to end slavery, but because of the Fugitive Slave Act, passed in September of 1850, Box Brown was no longer safe, even in the North. After Box and J. C. A. Smith, a free black man, were almost captured in Rhode Island, they fled to England. There, Box Brown continued to give speeches, display his panorama, called "Mirror of Slavery," and the famous box, and sell his books. Box Brown, and James C. A. "Boxer" Smith became partners and took his panorama and the box to theaters. The two men lectured to audiences about the evils of slavery. Box Brown also sang hymns and spirituals, and even shipped himself in a similar box, just for show, from Bradford to Leeds.

Box Brown's panorama, probably eight feet high and 500 feet long, had forty-nine scenes painted on canvases that were stitched together and wound on a vertical spool. The panorama would be unrolled in front of an audience, like a slide show, and rolled back up on another spool. Panoramas were a popular form or type of entertainment at the time and some were advertised as being as much as four miles long. Admission was twenty-five cents.

Eventually, Brown became famous as a professional entertainer. He often dressed as an African prince, and delighted audiences as a magician and the "King of all Mesmerisers" in Great Britain. In 1875, he returned to the United States with his second wife, and their daughter, Annie, and performed magic tricks with hats, hypnosis, cards, electricity, and boxes.

His advertisements referred to him as "Prof. H. Box Brown."

Historians haven't yet discovered when or where he died.

Jeffrey Ruggles' *The Unboxing of Henry Brown* provides fascinating details in the life of this amazing man, and those who helped him. Ruggles writes: "[Box Brown] was who he had made himself to be."

In 1996, historian Anthony Cohen, who has retraced various routes of the Underground Railroad, shipped himself in a box from Philadelphia to New York City to see what it was like.

In 2011, the Virginia Department of Historic Resources voted to install an historic marker in memory of Henry Box Brown, near where he was born and raised in Louisa County. It was placed near The Hermitage and dedicated in May 2012.

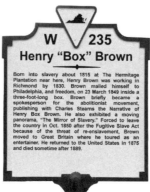

W 235
Henry "Box" Brown

Born into slavery about 1815 at The Hermitage Plantation near here, Henry Brown was working in Richmond by 1830. Brown mailed himself to Philadelphia, and freedom, on 23 March 1849 inside a three-foot-long box. Brown briefly became a spokesperson for the abolitionist movement, publishing with Charles Stearns the Narrative of Henry Box Brown. He also exhibited a moving panorama, "The Mirror of Slavery." Forced to leave the country in Oct. 1850 after the Fugitive Slave Act because of the threat of re-enslavement, Brown moved to Great Britain where he toured as an entertainer. He returned to the United States in 1875 and died sometime after 1889.

The original part of The Hermitage, the plantation home of Henry Brown, was built in 1725, and was expanded in about 1800 to what it looks like today. He and his family probably lived behind the main house in the kitchen building, which no longer exists. Kitchens were often located in a separate building to protect the main house from fire.

The little Trevilians one-room school house, used from 1880–1922 for up to grade six, was relocated to Mineral, Virginia.

REPRESENTATION OF THE BOX,

In which a fellow mortal travelled a long journey, in quest of those rights which the piety and republicanism of this country denied to him, the right to possess.

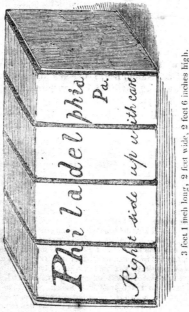

3 feet 1 inch long, 2 feet wide, 2 feet 6 inches high.

As long as the temples of humanity contain a single worshipper, whose heart beats in unison with that of the God of the universe; must a religion and a government which could inflict such misery upon a human being, be execrated and fled from, as a bright angel, abhors and flees from the touch of hideous sin.

Illustration from page 92 of Henry Box Brown's narrative, 1849. Used with permission, Documenting the American South.

Glossary

banana lumpia: A Filipino appetizer like a spring roll.

beaver hut: A lodge or home that beavers make out of sticks and brush at the edge of the water.

bilis: "Hurry" or "speed" in Tagalog, a language spoken in the Philippines. Flora was born and raised in the Philippines, then moved to Guam and married Paul Fish.

bladder: A sack probably from an animal, that could contain liquids.

crappie: A freshwater fish.

docket: A list of legal cases for the court.

gimlet: A small screwlike tool for boring holes.

guardian ad litem: A person appointed to represent a child, such as a foster child.

halo-halo: A popular Filipino dessert made with shredded ice, fruit pieces, cooked beans, coconut milk and sugar, served in a tall glass and topped with ice cream or flan.

narrative: A story that is told.

Acknowledgments

A very special thank you to the families who shared their earthquake experiences to make this book real, especially: Abigale, Isabelle, and Shanna Hart; Lindsey Hottinger; Chrissie, Maggie, and Mitchell McCotter; Emma, Savannah, and Ryan Lyle, and Brenda Anderson.

I'm also deeply indebted to Elaine Taylor, director of the Louisa County Historical Society's Sargeant Museum. She provided leads and invaluable research material on historic earthquakes in Virginia, and introduced me to Henry Box Brown through a program by Anthony Cohen presented by the Louisa Historic Society. The coincidence of the earthquake and Brown's birthplace being in the same location became an irresistible part of this story.

Thanks also to Dr. Deborah Pettit, Louisa County school superintendent, for reviewing the portions that related specifically to the schools and giving me a tour of the sixth-grade hall where Bailey would have been that day. And to Jack Maus, an attorney who has handled adoptions in Louisa County. Also to Virginia Tech's Martin C. Chapman, PhD, and associate professor of Geophysics for information on the Mineral earthquake.

And to the everyone who read drafts of the book with suggestions and encouragement or for accuracy: My husband, Jim, Nancy Miller (a former teacher, who develops the discussion questions); Abbie Grotke; Julie Franklin; Shanna Hart; Bert and Barbara Stafford; Jack and Linda Maus, and Anthony Cohen.

And to the many readers who immediately after the earthquake insisted that Bailey needed to experience it in a new book. They included students at Byrd Elementary School in Goochland, who had ideas about how the book should be written, and homeschoolers in Fredericksburg, who helped select the title.

And as always, to Amber.

About the Author

 Linda Salisbury draws her inspiration for the Bailey Fish Adventure series from her experiences in Florida and Virginia, and as a mother, grandmother, mentor, and former foster mother. She is a musician and enjoys reading, boating, traveling and the family cats.

Also in the Bailey Fish Adventure series are: *The Wild Women of Lake Anna,* a *ForeWord* magazine finalist for Book of the Year 2005; *No Sisters Sisters Club,* silver finalist in Florida Publishers Association's Best Children's Fiction 2008; *The Thief at Keswick Inn* (winner of the FPA, President's Pick Award 2007); *The Mysterious Jamestown Suitcase* (gold medal for Best Children's Fiction in the 2009 FPA President's Book Awards, a bronze medalist in the Moonbeam Children's Book Awards, and *ForeWord* finalist); *Ghost of the Chicken Coop Theater;* and *Trouble in Contrary Woods* (finalist in the Eric Hoffer awards) and *Captain Calliope and the Great Goateenies. Treasure in Sugar's Book Barn* received a silver medal in the Moonbeam Children's Book Awards in the best juvenile fiction category, was an Eric Hoffer awards finalist, and took top honors for best children's fiction from the Virginia Press Women's Association.

Of special honor, Indiana Public Radio's StoryBoard, an excellent program for young listeners, selected *Ghost of the Chicken Coop Theater* to be read on air in the fall of 2013. Episodes are archived for listening at bsu.edu/ipr.storyboard.com beginning with S2Ep1.

Salisbury is also the author of *Mudd Saves the Earth: Booger Glue, Cow Diapers and Other Good Ideas* (an FPA silver medalist), plus humorous books for "grown-ups." Read more about them at www.lindasalisburyauthor.com.

About the Illustrator

 Illustrator and book designer Carol Tornatore lives in Nokomis, Florida, with her Siamese cats. She has won numerous awards for her innovative book and magazine designs. Some of her other children's books include *Florida A to Z, The Runaway Bed, Zachary Cooks Up Some Fun*, and the *Southern Fossil Discovery* series. She enjoys going to the beach, collecting sea shells, and dancing.